VEGAN RECIPES *for* NEW AGE MEN

VEGAN RECIPES
for
NEW AGE MEN

LIZ TREACHER

SKELBO

First published in the UK in 2023
by SKELBO Press
Tollich, Skelbo, Dornoch, IV25 3QQ
www.skelbopress.com

ISBN: 978-1-8380383-3-5

Edited by Lottie Fyfe
Cover design and typesetting by Raspberry Creative Type.

for Lucie & Catalin

DISCLAIMER

Nash Adderman is not as good a chef as he thinks he is. Readers should approach his recipes with extreme caution! I hope that you will enjoy his jokes, but disregard all his instructions.

CONTENTS

London, 2015   1

Chapter 1   3

Chapter 2   9

Chapter 3   21

Chapter 4   41

Chapter 5   49

Chapter 6   71

Chapter 7   82

Chapter 8   94

Chapter 9   99

Chapter 10   109

Chapter 11   133

Chapter 12   154

Chapter 13   169

Epilogue   185

Acknowledgements   187

About the Author   188

LONDON, 2015

CHAPTER 1

It's a day like any other. Cold and wet. The pavements in central London are shiny and rain is spurting out of the gutters as if the city doesn't know what to do with so much water. But the trees seem glad. As Lauren crosses Euston Square Gardens and turns towards the station, she can feel the horse chestnuts silently drinking it in.

The concourse outside the station is quiet and the chairs in front of the café are empty. Lauren peers through the steamed-up window. A couple of teenagers are huddling near the door and an older woman is ordering at the counter. Then Lauren spies another figure, right at the back. A tall man sitting with his back against the wall. She pushes the door open and goes inside.

Nash. A strange name. But she's had stranger. Her holiday let attracts all sorts, especially New Age types. She's also had a Zane and a Beckett.

I'm called Nash, he had said in his first email. And then, *It's Old English for 'cliff'.* Old English and New Age. Interesting how the two seemed to go together, the *now* and the *then* curling round to join each other, ignoring all those vital bits in the middle like central heating and penicillin.

New Age tenants were usually full of questions before they decided to let. They asked if the house was stocked with Ecover and whether Lauren's business was carbon neutral. But Nash had asked more questions than usual. A whole lot more. He wanted to know about stone circles and ley lines; about nesting birds and bats. When it transpired that they both lived in London, Lauren suggested that it might be easier if they met for a quick coffee, the emphasis on the *quick*.

As she walks through the café towards him, Lauren notices that the man's eyes are closed. They stay shut as she reaches his table and sits down in the chair opposite.

He looks just like what her grandmother would call a 'hippy'. Mousy hair tied back in a bushy ponytail and a massive beard. A denim shirt and jeans cut off at the knee revealing long, tanned legs. He is wearing flip flops, which feels completely wrong for the weather. Lauren glances at his feet and notices dark hairs sprouting out of the toes.

'Nash?'

The man's eyes remain closed but he puts one hand up, like a priest blessing a parishioner. 'I need a moment,' he says. 'I have to come down slowly.'

Lauren waits until he opens his eyes. 'Nash?' she asks again. But it's obviously him – who else can it be? Only a man named after a cliff would sit meditating in a coffee shop and wear flip flops in the rain.

'Lauren?'

She doesn't reply. Two can play at that game.

'You own the house in Door Knock?'

'It's a cottage. And it's not in Dornoch. It's further north. Beside Loch Fleet.'

'Lock Fleet?' asks Nash.

'*Loch* Fleet,' replies Lauren.

'That's what I said. Lock.'

'It's a sea loch,' continues Lauren. 'The tide comes in and out.'

'I see.' Nash unfolds a scrap of paper lying on the table beside him – a printout from the booking agency's page about the cottage – and reads it. '*Fois*, Loch Fleet.' He looks at Lauren. 'What does *Fois* mean?'

He's pronounced it *foyz*, but Lauren doesn't correct him this time. 'It's the name of the cottage. It's Gaelic for peace,' she replies.

'And is it?'

'Is it what?'

'Your house. Is it peaceful?'

'It's not a house, it's a cottage. Besides, shouldn't I be interviewing you?' Lauren can feel anger rising in her throat. She's no longer sure that she wants Nash to stay. She pictures him standing barefoot on her white wooden floorboards and glances again at his hairy toes.

'It's important,' Nash explains. 'For my book.'

'I'm sorry?'

'I'm writing a book and I need a place with the right...' Nash pauses and waves his hands around.

Don't say it, please don't say it.

'...Feng shui.'

'Did you look at the pictures on the website?' Lauren asks.

'Not all of them.' A pause. 'The view seemed nice.'

'It's a cottage with a nice view. If that's not *feng shui* enough for you, maybe you should holiday elsewhere.'

'It's not a holiday. Writing is hard work.'

'Whatever.' Lauren stands up and slings her bag over her shoulder in a take-it-or-leave-it kind of way. *Leave it*, she prays silently. *Please leave it.*

'I'll take it!' Nash gives her a triumphant grin as if he has just awarded her first prize in a competition. His teeth, she notices, are perfect. White, regular and just the right size. A smile from a toothpaste advert. It makes him even more annoying, somehow.

'Fine.' Lauren mutters and turns away. As she walks back to the door, she hears him add, 'I can sort out the *feng shui* when I get there.'

Thank God for Patrick. And Lauren does. Regularly. She's always sneaking into the back of churches full of headscarved ladies and dusty-looking nuns, slipping into the pew beside them and bowing her head. Lauren's not really religious, but Patrick is a big deal. And precious things need some sort of insurance policy. She's lucky to have him and she needs to keep luck on her side. She'd do the same thing if she was a gambler, or regularly swimming with sharks.

Patrick is outside the station in his Jaguar, waiting to whisk Lauren off to a friend's house for dinner. Lauren experiences the usual feeling of butterflies at the sight of him. He looks really smart, dressed in a cream jacket and a white shirt, and Lauren is glad she is wearing a linen dress and her new leather sandals. She'd wanted to just fling on some jeans, but Patrick's friends aren't into casual. And nor is Patrick. *Don't rush,* Lauren tells herself as she hurries towards the car.

'You look great!' he says. 'Good day?'

'Yes, and thank you!'

It's their little joke, answering things in the wrong order; the thing they do as a couple that makes Lauren laugh and Patrick smile. Some of her friends have much jokier boyfriends, but they're not lawyers like Patrick. Being a lawyer is a serious profession. Patrick takes it seriously, anyway.

Patrick's perfect. Dark, curly hair, large bright eyes, a lovely smile and immaculate taste in clothes. He's also got the three Rs: reliable, reputable, respectable. And that means a lot.

Because Patrick's a lawyer, all his friends are lawyers too. Lauren usually feels out of her depth with them, but tonight she makes everyone laugh by recounting her encounter with Nash. She even embellishes things to make the story better, adding hairs to Nash's nose, as well as his toes. As his friends laugh, Lauren can see how pleased Patrick is with her and this makes her exaggerate even more.

Their hostess for the evening is Veronica. She works alongside Patrick. Veronica is an attractive woman with fair hair cut in a short, shiny bob. She is also tall and very skinny, perhaps because she cooks such tiny dinners. Tonight's offering is a pocket-sized piece of steak and roasted veg. Not a potato in sight. Lauren would have liked a potato; a potato would have filled her up. Or even better, chips. *Nouvelle cuisine*. That's what Veronica calls it. But Lauren is sure that *nouvelle* means new, not small.

'What a pity you have to rent out your cottage,' says Veronica after Lauren has finished her story.

'Indeed.' Lauren spends a lot of time trying to like Veronica. She's Patrick's colleague and also his friend, so she must have some good points.

'Wouldn't it be marvellous, having somewhere to shoot off to for the weekend?' Veronica's eyes rove round the table, catching Patrick's before moving on.

'Inverness is quite a long way for the weekend,' Lauren ventures.

'But surely there's a plane from Heathrow?'

Lauren can't afford to fly to Inverness from Heathrow; she has to take EasyJet from Luton, but she smiles at Veronica anyway. Fitting in. Lauren spends her whole life doing it. Or trying to. Most of the time she feels as if she's jumped into the deep end of the swimming pool. She can't touch the bottom; all she can do is tread water. She looks calm and smiling, but under the surface she's doing a crazy sort of doggy-paddle just to keep afloat.

'You did well tonight,' Patrick says, as he and Lauren walk back to the car. 'Your story about the hippy was hilarious!'

'Thank you.'

'They really like you,' he adds, as he carefully reverses

out from a tight spot between a Range Rover and a Porsche.

This is always Lauren's favourite bit of the evening. The bit when they are in the car going home, leaving all Patrick's friends behind. She leans her head back against the headrest, opens the window and lets the night air fly in.

Lauren loves driving through London after dark. There are fewer cars on the roads and the quiet city streets remind her of the Nineties, when London was less frenetic. She shuts her eyes and remembers driving with her mother at night, sailing past a deserted Trafalgar Square, the lions white and majestic in the moonlight. What would her mother have made of Veronica? Or even Patrick? She would have disapproved, probably. *Reliable, reputable, respectable.* Her mother was none of those things.

They turn into Prince of Wales Road and Regents Park opens up on their left. Lauren feels like asking Patrick to stop the car so they can walk up Primrose Hill and look out at the city from the top. She swallows the idea down and visualises the view instead: London spread beneath the hill like a sparkling tablecloth.

Bizarrely, Nash springs into her mind. She pictures him leaping towards the summit in a meditative trance, and starts to worry that he might not look after her cottage. She imagines him filling the bath with seaweed or digging a firepit in the garden.

But when they are back at Patrick's flat, and he opens the bedroom window onto the patio and makes a pot of Lapsang Souchong, Lauren stops worrying about Nash. She takes in Patrick's clean-shaven face, his curly hair and his Paisley dressing gown. Now they are away from his friends, he is concentrating on her. Lauren feels so glad that *she* is the one he's pouring tea for. He hands her a cup and smiles. His eyes shine. She could do this for ever, she realises. Sipping tea; whispering in the darkness. Outside, the patter of rain and the purring of a passing car. And she thanks God for Patrick.

CHAPTER 2

If he had read the small print in the information about the holiday let, or looked it up on Google Maps, Nash would have known that Dornoch was a long, long way from London. But he hadn't. So it's only when he arrives at King's Cross and gets on the midday train to Inverness that he realises he will be stuck on it until eight o'clock that evening. And he doesn't have sandwiches. *No worries*, he tells himself, *there'll be a buffet*.

The buffet, which doesn't open until York, is not as environmentally friendly as Nash would have hoped. When he asks the woman behind the counter what there is for vegans, she points to an egg and cress sandwich. Nash looks at his watch. Half past two in the afternoon. He swiftly calculates what would be the bigger ecological disaster, an egg eaten or a dead vegan, and decides the latter is worse. He buys the sandwich and returns to his seat. The packaging, which doesn't look compostable, claims the eggs are from Cornwall. The train is nearly at Newcastle now, which means the carbon footprint of the eggs is already immense. He wolfs the sandwich quickly before their mileage increases.

The sandwich is surprisingly salty and, as soon as he finishes it, Nash feels a great thirst. There is absolutely no chance of him buying a plastic bottle of water. Oh no. Not him. Never.

He gets to his feet and sways along the corridor to the toilet. To his horror, a sign above the tap says: NOT FOR DRINKING. Again Nash is faced with a life-or-death choice. And again, he chooses life. He returns to the buffet and buys a large bottle of Highland Spring. It sounds Scottish and he is, after all, going to Scotland. It's only when he gets back to his seat that he realises the water has already travelled all the way from Scotland to London and is now heading back again.

Nash bends his head over the bottle and says a little prayer. He prays that the plastic will not end up on a ship to China but will be effectively recycled into a bag or a T-shirt. And while he's at it, he prays for the chickens, too. The ones that so generously sacrificed their eggs, life sustaining life in a beautiful circle, if not exactly a vegan one.

Soon after Newcastle the train lurches towards the coast and the view out of the window becomes spectacular. Nash feasts his eyes on rugged cliffs which drop down to crashing waves below.

And then they have crossed the border into Scotland, and each station sits in a more dramatic landscape than the last. Stirling with its hilltop monuments and castle; Perth with its lush green fields and enormous trees; Dalwhinnie and the first glimpse of the Cairngorm mountains covered with grazing deer. *Life is a journey, not a destination.* Who said that? Nash looks it up on his phone. Ah, Emerson. Another quote for the book. Now he doesn't care how long his journey takes. Even when he gets off at Inverness and discovers that if he wants to continue on to Dornoch he will have to take a bus. Because the bus takes him over three different bridges that span vast stretches of water. The Moray Firth, the Cromarty Firth and, finally, the Dornoch Firth. Each more beautiful than the last.

Eventually, the bus turns off the main road and into a

small town. Large, old-fashioned houses line the road. Every house seems to have a secret garden hidden behind high stone walls. They pass a hotel that looks like a castle, and a sandstone cathedral. Then the bus pulls up beside a wooden bus shelter.

Nash picks up his rucksack and lumbers up to the front. 'Is this Door Knock?'

'Dornoch,' says the driver. 'The last stop.'

'I thought you might be going on to Lock Fleet?'

'No, but it's nae far to walk.'

'How far?'

'Och, just a couple of miles. You won't mind a wee stroll on such a lovely night.'

'Night?'

'Aye. It's almost ten.'

Nash has never worn a watch. He likes to tell the time by the sun. And he's one of those people that can guess the hour, more or less, within a few minutes. But he would never have imagined it could be nearly ten o'clock with the sky so light.

'Which way to the lock?'

'You mean the loch?' The driver laughs and points to the other end of town. 'Follow the road. Keep the sea on your right. Carry on past the barley fields and then down the hill.'

Nash is glad of the walk. After racing up the country by train, there is something nice about putting the brakes on at the end. He slings his rucksack over his shoulder and takes the road out of town. The sea appears almost immediately. The sun has gone, but the water is light blue, reflecting the last of its light. He passes the barley fields and then turns down a hill lined with trees. Under the canopy of leaves, the sky is darker and he feels the swoop of bats.

Once out of the trees, Nash sees the loch below him, pale silver in colour. On his side of the loch there are fields full of sheep. Nestled between the fields and the water is a cottage.

Home, Nash thinks, *for a week anyway*. And his heart leaps.

The light is finally fading and, by the time he arrives, the moss-covered gate to the cottage is a little fuzzy around the edges. Even in the twilight, the cottage looks sweet. A single-storey building, covered with white harling. Long and low, it looks like a converted byre, with windows and a porch added much later, in the seventies perhaps.

Nash pushes the gate open and drags his rucksack up the path to the front entrance. The key is exactly where what's her name said it would be, hidden in a crack under the doorstep. He slots it into the lock.

Inside the porch, the air is warm and stale. Nash walks through the cottage, flinging the doors of the different rooms open and peering inside. A dark corridor leads to an open-plan kitchen-cum-living room with French windows looking onto decking. Beyond it, he finds three bedrooms and a bathroom.

Back in the kitchen, Nash checks the contents of the cupboards. Food processor? Yep. Liquidiser? Yep. Grinder? Nope. No grinder. So how will he grind his walnuts?

At the back of one of the cupboards he discovers a dusty-looking bottle. Whisky. Malt whisky! Nash pours himself a generous measure and takes it out onto the decking.

The sky has finally darkened, but he knows there is water nearby because he can hear waves lapping on the shoreline. 'Hello lock!' he calls. He tries again. 'Lochhhh!'

A startled Eider duck takes off in fright, its wings furiously beating the air. Nash grins apologetically and takes a swig of his malt. As he swills the peaty whisky around his mouth, he remembers her name. *Lauren*. It's easy to remember her face. A mass of chestnut hair – long and wavy – and piercing green eyes. And even if he hadn't met her, he could have sensed her here.

There are clues about her all over the place. The dried-up house plants crammed into pots that are much too small for them; the lack of family photos. A long, knitted scarf hanging on a hook by the back door which looks as if it has shrunk in the wash. And in every room, touches of the same colour – a bright bluey-green. From the towels in the bathroom and the kitchen curtains to the china mugs and the shower mat.

Nash doesn't believe in ghosts, but he believes in auras, and Lauren's is decidedly turquoise. Throat-chakra turquoise. The colour of communication – or lack of it. Which one, he wonders, applies to her?

* * *

When Lauren's mother died, far too young at twenty-eight, she left Lauren two things. A cottage beside a sea loch and a grandmother. And both became vital for Lauren's well-being. The cottage provided a rental income, and Granny provided a home.

Granny lived in a crumbling house in Croydon. A Victorian pile that she bought for a song back in the early 1960s. It was a great place for Lauren to grow up because it had a lovely garden. Rows of raspberries, an orchard of fruit trees and stepping stones over a scruffy lawn.

Lauren was a solitary child, and the garden became her best friend. She used to hit a tennis ball for hours against the garden wall. She built a den under the plum tree and did hundreds of handstands on the lumpy lawn. Sometimes she just lay on the grass, squinting out at the sun through half-closed eyelids.

Granny was born before the Second World War and, like all babies born at that time, she was programmed in the womb to think solely about bargains, the good old days and the price of butter. She even had an old-fashioned name: Amelia. And she lived up to it. Amelia could darn socks, take up curtains and turn the collar of a shirt so that Lauren got twice the wear out of it. She could make crumbles and pies, briskets and biscuits.

Not anymore of course. At eighty-five, she has retired from all types of mending and most forms of cooking, although she still bottles fruit from her garden. Once the blackcurrants are finished, Granny lives on heated-up scones and tins of baked beans. Nowadays she spends her time summoning Lauren to Croydon to do chores for her. Chores that she loves to supervise.

This week's chores are firstly to vacuum the house, and then to de-spider it. Granny always has two or three spiders lurking in the bathroom where they spin industrial-sized webs, but they've been busy on her stairs as well. Lauren's job is to destroy their workmanship. She has to stand halfway up the stairs, armed only with a broom, and pull down a web that stretches from floor to ceiling. Granny intends to watch her do it.

'Stop hovering!' Lauren brandishes the broom at her. 'I'm not going to do it if you stand there.'

Granny gives Lauren the eye and returns to the telly.

Up until recently, Granny has always been in charge. But now they're both getting older, the who's-in-charge thing is becoming more fluid. Lauren's weekly visits to Croydon are not just to do chores; she's also here to check. Check there aren't any mice in Granny's bedroom and that there's nothing mouldy at the back of her fridge. So, at this precise moment in time, they are both supervising each other in a tug-of-war kind of way.

Lauren's mobile pings and she pulls it out of her pocket. It's a WhatsApp from Nash. A picture of her bathroom in the Highlands with water all over the floor. The accompanying text reads: ONLY ONE BATHROOM!

Why are you telling me that? Lauren frowns at the puddles on the wooden floor.

Another ping. This time it's a picture of a pair of brown legs lying on the beach. Ten toes are sticking up, partially obscuring the view of the loch. The feet are in silhouette so the toe hairs are not visible. This time the text reads LOOKING FORWARD TO A TROUBLE-FREE WEEK!

'How's it going?' calls Granny from the sitting room.

Lauren puts down the phone and returns to the task in hand.

As she attacks the spider's webs, Lauren imagines Nash sitting on the beach looking out at the waves and feels a pang of jealousy. Why does he get to relax at Loch Fleet while she is stuck in Croydon, making spiders homeless?

You need the money, she tells herself. But another part of her brain is trying to calculate how long it has been since she escaped to Scotland. Not last summer. Not the year before that, because she and Patrick blew their annual leave on a trip to Tuscany. How lovely it would be to get away.

Lauren puts down the broom, picks up her phone and flicks to the calendar on the holiday home's website. This week is taken by Nash, but the rest of July and the whole of August is free. The booking agency allows Lauren to use the house for up to ten weeks a year. She never does, of course. She needs the income. But if the cottage is going to be empty anyway... A plan starts to form in her head. She goes back through to the living room.

'Granny,' she says, as if the idea has just occurred to her. 'Do you remember when Felicity is coming over from the States?'

'Goddaughter Felicity?' Granny replies, keeping her eyes on the news.

'Yes. When is she coming to stay with you?'

'August.'

'Early in the month, or later?'

'Saturday the eighth, I think. Staying till the twenty-second.'

Lauren glances at the calendar on her phone. With someone here to keep an eye on Granny, she could take off and have a holiday.

'Felicity prefers it when you're around.'

Granny is a mind-reader.

'Oh, I will be,' Lauren smiles. 'For her second week.' She has just chopped her holiday in half.

'We could always go to Scotland with you,' Granny suggests, keeping her psychic hat on.

'No! I mean... I think I need a bit of a break.'

'From me?'

'From everything.'

'And is Patrick going?'

'I don't know yet.'

'I doubt it.' Having made her gloomy prediction, Granny turns off the telly. 'I've just remembered another job for you,' she says. 'In the garage.'

* * *

When she isn't looking after her grandmother, Lauren has another career. She works as a proofreader for Jerbil, a niche publisher in Edgware. She makes sure that everything they publish is absolutely perfect. And she's good at it.

The only problem is that her job is not really nine to five. Because Lauren has a voice in her head, a proofreading voice that never stops, and this means she can never escape her occupation. She proofreads every word that enters her life. Newspapers, magazines, junk mail, a note from the neighbour; Lauren's grammatical eye is always at work. She can't watch foreign films because she gets too distracted by the subtitles. She misses the action because she's concentrating on the text, moving apostrophes and adding full stops.

It's Friday lunchtime and most of the office have gone out to celebrate the launch of *Death by Dalmadoodle*, the fourth book in their cosy crime series, leaving Camilla the receptionist and Lauren in charge.

Camilla is the most exciting person at Jerbil Publishing. She has amazing hair, cropped at the sides and bushy and floppy on top, and it's always dyed an interesting colour. At the moment it's blue, an electric blue that makes Lauren's chestnut curls feel dull in comparison.

'So, are you going away anywhere this summer?' Camilla fishes her Earl Grey teabag out of her cup and balances it on her saucer.

'*Scot*land,' Lauren emphasises the first syllable to try and make her holiday sound adventurous.

'Your cottage?'

'Yes!' Lauren laughs with relief at no longer having to pretend she is going anywhere exotic. 'I love it there.'

'Why? It can't be the weather?'

'No.'

'What then?'

'It's...' Lauren hesitates. What was it that she loved? 'It's the space,' she says eventually.

'Space?'

'You know, the fact that you can see for miles from the house, the sea to the east, the loch to the north and the mountains to the west.'

'So it's the view?'

'Not just the view. It's being able to walk on the beach for hours without meeting anyone.'

'Isn't that a bit lonely?'

'No.' A shadow of doubt crosses Lauren's mind. 'I think Patrick will come.'

'You mean he might not?'

'I'm not sure.' Lauren doesn't want to admit she hasn't asked him yet.

'How long have you guys been together now?'

'Oh, about three years.'

'In for the long-term, then?'

'Yes.' Lauren looks around for some wood to touch.

'Funny, he's never been to our Christmas party.'

'No. He... um, well... he works long hours.'

'At Christmas?'

'He's a lawyer,' replies Lauren, as if that explains everything.

'Right.' Camilla looks thoughtful for a moment, then she smiles.

* * *

Patrick is just doing up his laces when his phone rings. He glances at the caller and flips the mobile onto speakerphone: 'Lauren! I know I'm late. Leaving any sec.'

'It's just the casserole is drying up.'

'Take it out of the oven. I'm only ten minutes away.'

'Don't forget, you said you'd get pudding.'

'Did I?' The two bows are not the same size. Patrick sighs and bends down to undo the laces and start again. 'I don't suppose you could pop out and get something? I'll be back quicker if I don't have to go to the shops.'

'Um… well, I could. I'm in my pyjamas.'

'Oh.' The bows are perfect now. Patrick gets to his feet.

'But of course, I can easily get dressed again. You've had such a long day.'

'I have.' As he speaks Patrick smiles at Veronica and gives her a little wave. 'You're a brick, Lauren. I'll be home very soon.'

* * *

When he was still a trainee lawyer, Patrick was warned that he could occasionally look rather blank when he talked to clients. It was explained to him that people wanted their solicitor to express a certain amount of emotion. Since then Patrick has worked hard to improve his facial expressions, particularly the expression of regret.

'I'm so sorry.' As he looks at Lauren over the supper table, Patrick can feel his eyes go soft and shiny. 'I can't come. You see, our office AGM is always the second Monday in August.'

'What if I made it the following week?'

'No. I think you should go as soon as possible. Don't wait for me. You need to get away.'

'Couldn't you just come for a few days?'

Patrick reaches over the tiramisu and takes Lauren's hand. 'Why don't we go away together when you get back. Cornwall perhaps?'

'I can't. I'll have to spend time with Felicity.'

'After she's gone, then?'

Lauren nods.

'I'm sorry. I would have loved to come. It's just the timing's all wrong.' Patrick lets go of Lauren's hand and touches the back of her neck.

'Granny said you wouldn't come.'

Patrick swallows his irritation. 'Your grandmother doesn't know me.'

'That's not her fault.'

'I don't like to intrude on your visits. I know she wants to spend time with *you*.' A pause. 'It's great you're so close to her.'

'She's all I've got.'

You've got me. The words form in his mind but Patrick can't get them out of his mouth. Terrible how he knows what he should say, but he can't always say it. The silence grows.

'I need to go to bed.' Patrick gets up from the table. 'You'll have a great time up north, Lauren. It's just what you need.'

* * *

The thing Patrick has noticed about truth is that it is not very stable. What may be true at one moment can become untrue the next. Like the tide going in and out, honesty and deceit go up and down, depending on the phases of the moon.

So when he gets an email the next morning to regretfully inform him that the AGM has been postponed, Patrick decides that he has not deceived Lauren. After all, when he told her he couldn't go to Loch Fleet, he really couldn't go. The fact that things have changed *now* doesn't alter the veracity of what he said *then*.

He and Lauren don't need to be together all the time. In fact, a break from each other is probably just what they need. Breaks are healthy. He'll miss her while she's away, of course he will. And she's bound to miss him too. She always does.

CHAPTER 3

There is something magical about leaving the muggy heat of London and landing in Inverness. It's usually about ten degrees cooler, and tonight is no exception. Lauren glances round at the other disembarking travellers as they wrap their jackets closer, then she takes a huge gulp of the evening air.

Lauren has persuaded Sian, her housekeeper, to meet her and drive her up to *Fois*. She's ordered a supermarket shop which should arrive tomorrow, and she's going to try and last the week without a car.

Sian is waiting in the carpark with her boot open, waving madly. Lauren dashes over, pulling her suitcase.

'Quick!' cries Sian. 'I've been here nine minutes now. If we get to the barrier in the next sixty seconds, I won't have to pay for the ticket.'

At the exit, the barrier opens obediently and they sail through.

And soon they are flying along the A9 towards Dornoch, ripening barley fields on either side of the car and, beyond the barley, glimpses of the Cromarty Firth opening out under an enormous sky.

'It's so great to be back,' Lauren sighs.

'Great to have you back!' smiles Sian. 'He's a laugh, that boyfriend of yours.'

'Patrick?' Lauren blushes with happiness. 'Thank you!' She feels relieved. When he and Sian met three years ago, Patrick had behaved in rather a standoffish manner.

'I don't mean *him*,' Sian says, in a way that suggests she doesn't consider Patrick to be much of a laugh. 'I mean Nash.'

'Nash isn't my boyfriend. Good heavens no!' It comes out in a rush. 'He's a holidaymaker. *Was* a holidaymaker.'

'Oh.' Sian looks puzzled. 'Right.'

After that they talk about other things, but it feels a bit awkward. Lauren wants to ask about Nash's stay, whether he left a mess and whether there were any breakages, but something stops her. She makes a mental note never to let to him again.

When they arrive at Loch Fleet, Sian drives off into the twilight and Lauren turns towards the cottage. The sitting room light is on and Lauren is not surprised to find the front door open. She pictures Sian coming in earlier, opening up, giving everything a quick dust and, realising that it might be dusk when they arrive, turning on the light.

There are surprising changes in the porch. Everything seems to be green. Enormously tall plants with large, luscious leaves jostle for room at the windows, filling the porch with a verdant hue. First Lauren thinks the plants are new, then she realises that they are the same plants she has always had, but that someone has re-potted them and they have taken off. Not just taken off, they've gone mad. Really mad. In fact it's quite hard to get through the porch now. Lauren pushes her way through the plants and into the living room.

And there, in the glow of a single table lamp, sitting on her sofa with a plastered leg resting on the coffee table, is a man. A Nash, to be precise. Lauren would have recognised him anywhere. The thick beard, which looks longer and bushier, the denim jeans slashed at the knee, and a single flip flop dangling from the foot without the plaster. Lauren drops her suitcase on the floor. 'What the hell!'

'Dear God,' Nash replies, looking up. 'Dear, dear God.' And then, 'You weren't in the calendar.'

Lauren can hardly believe her ears. 'Exactly which calendar are you referring to? The Druid calendar, the Viking calendar?'

'The one on the website.'

'You mean... you looked at the lettings calendar and thought, jeez, how lucky, there's no one coming for ages. I can outstay my welcome by, what, four weeks, five weeks?'

'Six.'

Nash's honesty makes Lauren angrier.

'Well, that's funny, because I didn't get your email asking to prolong your stay. Or your booking on the calendar. Or the payment for the booking.'

'I should have told you,' Nash looks stricken. 'I broke my leg and had to go to Casualty. I can't leave till next Saturday because I have a hospital appointment to take the plaster off.' He sees Lauren is unimpressed and adds, 'I bruised some ribs as well.'

'How?'

'How did I do it?

'Yes.'

'I fell out of the tree.'

'Tree?'

'The one in the garden.'

'The apple tree?'

'Yep.'

'Did you damage it?'

'No, I damaged *me*.'

'And what were you doing up a tree?'

'Communing.'

'So, let me get this straight. You climbed a tree – my tree – a tree that means a lot to me, incidentally, to *commune* with it, whatever that means. And you fell out and – abracadabra – became a squatter. Just like that.'

'It sounds worse than it is.'

'It's just not good enough, Nash. I've come for a holiday. A break from London, from work, from everything…'

'I'm sorry.'

'Not sorry enough to let me know.'

'I'll pay you back.'

'Too right you will.'

'I will. I promise. As soon as my book is published.'

'I thought you were still writing it?'

Nash doesn't reply.

'You mean it's not finished?'

'Not quite.'

'So what you're suggesting is more of a contribution to my pension plan than my cash flow?'

Nash looks away. 'I've let myself down,' he says.

'Yes, you have. And not just yourself. You've let me down, too.' Lauren picks up her suitcase and stalks out. She is suddenly exhausted. She needs to go to bed.

'I'll be gone on Saturday!' Nash calls after her.

'And I'll be gone on Sunday!' Lauren yells back. 'You bastard,' she adds under her breath.

Presuming that Nash will have commandeered the room she normally uses, Lauren veers into the bigger of the two spare bedrooms. A double bed is squeezed into the room at a funny angle perpendicular to the door, so that whoever is sleeping there has a view of the water. She pulls the curtain across and flops down on top of the bed. Too tired to undress, too tired even to clean her teeth. She closes her eyes.

* * *

At first light, Lauren is woken by a strange sound. On the loch there are usually only bird noises. The screech of oystercatchers, the croak of herons, the *ptit, ptit* of arctic terns. This sound is different, and it's coming from downstairs. A regular tapping, somewhere between a cling and a clang. A rushing sound ending in a crash. Lauren lies and listens. Then she hears another sound which is more recognisable. The sound of paper being dragged through something and screwed up. A typewriter. But of course – if Nash was writing a book, he would never use a computer; it would have to be a typewriter. The tapping starts again, but louder, more insistent. There'll be no chance of sleeping now. Lauren sighs and drags herself out of bed.

Nash is sitting at the dining table, bashing away on the keys. He is so engrossed in what he is doing he doesn't look up when Lauren comes in. She walks behind him and into the kitchen area. With the sun flooding in, the kitchen looks better than Lauren thought it would. There is lots of clutter on the surfaces, but they are clean at least, and the mugs are hanging where they should be on the hooks above the dresser. Lauren picks up the kettle and takes it over to the tap. The water comes out with a gush, soaking her sleeve. It feels icy cold. While she's waiting for the kettle to boil, Lauren opens the cupboard to hunt for coffee. None in sight, just packets and packets of herbal teas. She spies a jar of what looks like instant coffee tucked right at the back, but it turns out to be Barley Cup.

She leaves the kettle, wanders over to the bread bin and opens the lid. Inside is the charred remains of something. A loaf of bread so black it looks as if it might have been salvaged from the Great Fire of London. The paper it is wrapped in says *Charcoal Sourdough*. When Lauren picks the bread up to examine it, bits fall off onto the floor.

Curious now, she peers into the fridge. Bean burgers, sprouting seeds and a jar of liquid labelled 'aquafaba'. In other words, nothing edible. She looks inside the food cupboard. A tub of thick-looking peanut butter and a packet of cereal called Ancient Grains. Lauren finds a bowl and pours some in. The grains are the size of bird seed and twice as hard. They rattle into the bowl like ball bearings.

Lauren returns to the fridge to find some milk. There are three cartons to choose from: almond, soya or oat. No dairy. Of course no dairy. She tips the Ancient Grains back into the box, shuts the cupboard and goes outside.

And then she remembers why she came. The view this morning is spectacular – like walking into a picture book of sea and sky. From the decking Lauren can see the shore, the loch and the hills beyond. Curlews pick their way carefully across the shoreline, pecking for worms with their long, hooked beaks. Further out, a seal is dragging itself onto a sandbank. It looks as stubby as a stuffed stocking. Beyond the sandbank, the water stretches towards the mountains in a thin silver line. Everywhere, the smell and taste of seaweed.

Lauren puts on some wellies, throws a cardigan over her pyjamas and steps into the garden. She makes her way past the apple tree, over the rough ground that separates the house from the beach and jumps onto the shingle.

From the decking she could see the loch and the hills behind, but from the beach, the whole curve of the shoreline is visible. Lauren does a 180-degree turn, spinning on her wellingtons, taking in the heather-covered mountains where the loch ends, then following the water as it swells into a blue balloon, then narrows again as it flows out to sea.

There are mounds of white spume on the foreshore. They wobble madly like giant blobs of shaving foam. The sun gleams on the wet sand. When Lauren looks behind, the footprints of her boots have disappeared, swallowed completely by the silt.

Two seals swim past in parallel. Lauren watches them as they approach the funnel that joins the loch to the sea. When the tide turns, a current builds up there, creating a whirlpool that traps fish, making them easy pickings for the seals.

Suddenly the air is full of cries. A cluster of geese, black cut outs against the sky. They come closer, then slowly descend, parachuting downwards on outstretched wings like soldiers landing in enemy territory. Most geese migrate north for the summer, but a few of them stay behind, refusing to leave with the others. Lauren can understand them. Who in their right mind would want to leave this place?

* * *

When Lauren gets back to the cottage, Nash is in the kitchen. 'And how are you today?' he asks tentatively.

'In need of a coffee.'

'Caffeine is not that good for you, you know.'

'Let's not get into another argument.'

'Have you tried Barley Cup?'

Lauren pulls a face. 'And the place is a mess.'

'I would have tidied up, if I'd known you were coming.'

'You're transparent, Nash. I can see right through you.'

He smiles then. 'Like a jellyfish! I saw hundreds of them yesterday. On the beach.'

'How did you get onto the beach with your leg in plaster?'

'I found a walking stick. In the scullery.'

'Oh, yeah. That.'

'Is it yours?'

'No.'

'Whose, then?'

Lauren hesitates. 'It belonged to my mother.'

'Belonged?'

'Here's how things will work this week,' Lauren says, changing the subject. 'We will cook *all* our meals separately. We will use our own food, not each other's.'

'You don't like vegan?' he smiles.

Lauren ignores his comment and continues: 'I have groceries being delivered this morning. You will cook first. After you've cooked you will wash up and clear the kitchen, and you will respect my privacy while I'm cooking.'

'Can I write while you're cooking?'

'Only if it's in your room.' Lauren glances over at the battered-looking typewriter which takes up most of the dining table. It looks as if it has been run over by a lorry or dropped from a great height.

'It still works!' Nash smiles, as if he has read her mind. He gestures to a pile of papers lying beside it. The top page appears to be a title.

YORE WILDE SIDE: NASH'S GUIDE TO NEW AGE THINKING.

Yore Wilde Side! The typos are almost unbearable. 'Yore is spelt wrong,' Lauren begins.

'A play on words. Yore means the olden—'

'I know what it means, but it's confusing on a book cover. And Wilde—'

'Old English for untamed and uncontrolled.'

'Why not just put *Wild* with no 'e', it means the same thing.'

Nash shrugs. 'The publisher doesn't mind.'

'You have a publisher?'

'Yep.'

'British?'

'Nebraskan.'

'Called?'

'Before the Bear.'

Lauren imagines a couple of blokes in a log cabin, printing off the book as a Word document and stapling it together.

'And when it's published, I'll pay you back.'

'You said that yesterday.' Lauren looks again at the title. 'Anyway, even if the publisher doesn't mind your spelling, the proofreader will.'

'They won't.'

'Yes, they will. I'm a proofreader, I should know.'

'You're a proofreader?'

'Yes.'

Nash thinks for a minute. 'Perhaps I could call it *Falling out of a Tree: Nash's Guide to New Age Thinking*. Because I *did* fall from a tree...'

'Or just *Falling Out*,' Lauren says sarcastically.

'*Falling Out*,' muses Nash. 'It has a certain ring to it.'

Outside, there is the roar of a car engine, a squeal of breaks and then a man's voice: 'Post!'

Relieved to have an excuse to get away, Lauren hurries outside. Hamish, the local postie, is opening the doors of his van. His fair hair shines in the sun.

'Hi, Hamish!'

'Why, it's Lauren!' beams Hamish. 'Wonderful to see you.'

'And you! Can't believe you're still doing this!'

'I know. Ten years.'

'You'll be able to retire soon!'

'Not on these wages. Actually, I'm branching out. I mean, away from the job. Got a taxi now. Just at weekends, like.' He grins. 'Keeps the wolf from the door.'

'That's great! I hope it goes well.'

'Cross fingers. How's things with you?'

'Good!'

'And himself?'

'Who?'

'Nash. How's his leg?'

'You know Nash?'

'I know his baking,' Hamish grins. 'What a baker he is. I wish it was every day. Oh, don't forget your letter...'

* * *

The day continues in an awkward way. Nash and Lauren creep around each other in the kitchen. Lauren's groceries are delivered and she burns the pizza she'd planned to eat for lunch. Still, at least she has proper coffee now. Nash cooks something with mountains of garlic which looks awful but smells quite good. Lauren spends the afternoon sitting on the decking, thinking about Patrick and wishing she hadn't come.

As if things aren't bad enough, Granny's goddaughter Felicity starts emailing, complaining that there's nothing to see in London. All the art galleries are heaving with people. *What am I supposed to do?* Felicity asks. *You can't get near the paintings for the crowds. Also, when did Amelia become such a supervisor?* And then a nebulous question – *How far is Orkney from Dornoch?* Lauren has a terrible feeling that her holiday will be even more short-lived than she feared. It makes her even madder with Nash for ruining everything. She decides to go to bed very early and then wake up long before he does so she can have some peace and quiet.

* * *

When her alarm goes off at 6.30 the next morning, Lauren is initially confused. Then she remembers. This is her chance to enjoy her holiday. Alone. She opens the bedroom curtains. The sky is cloudy, but there are patches of light blue peeping through. The tide is going out, leaving large sandbanks behind. Between the sandbanks, water glitters.

Lauren gets out of bed and pokes her head out into the corridor. No sound from Nash's room. She gets dressed and tiptoes along to the kitchen.

The French windows are already open. Strange – she remembers closing them last night. Still, it means the kitchen feels lovely and cool. A tiny breeze makes its way around the room, fluttering the papers on the table.

As Lauren fills the kettle, she hears a low humming noise. Where is it coming from? She opens the fridge. Not from there. She tries the router. Still no. She cocks her head to one side and listens. The porch? She goes to investigate.

And there is Nash, standing in a T-shirt and boxers, hugging the plants. Well, not literally hugging. His arms are stretched out in a sort of socially-distanced hug, in the way a conductor embraces an orchestra. His eyes are closed and his lips are vibrating in a strange, continuous hum. But what is even stranger is that the plants are vibrating too, their leaves quivering as if in response.

'Reiki,' he says, without opening his eyes. At first Lauren thinks he is talking to the plants, then she realises he has heard her approach.

'Why?' It's a genuine question.

Nash lowers his arms and opens his eyes. 'They needed it.'

'Not anymore. I mean, look at them. If they get any bigger, they'll go through the ceiling. And what a peculiar noise!'

'Reiki is normally done silently,' Nash explains. 'But your plants seem to like it.'

Lauren glances at the plants. They look both exhausted and revitalised, as if they have had a deep tissue massage. There will be another growth spurt later.

'Well, you'll have to stop. Both the humming and the reiki. The porch isn't big enough.' And then suddenly Lauren starts to giggle. It's too surreal. Getting up at dawn to discover that Nash is turning the house plants into triffids. She sits down on the chair by the window and laughs outright. It feels like a release. And once she starts, she can't stop. Wait a minute – she's crying now: tears shooting out of her eyes like water from a burst pipe. She feels Nash approaching, sees his conductor's arms opening. *Oh no! No reiki for me.*

Lauren jumps up and wipes her nose with the back of her hand. 'Hay fever!' she says. 'Always gets me.' And she rushes back to the kitchen.

Nash doesn't follow; he leaves her in peace. He sits down in front of his typewriter again and continues to bash away at his book.

Lauren makes a coffee and carries it out to the decking. When she's finished drinking it, she lies on the sun lounger and closes her eyes.

Inside the kitchen, the tapping has been replaced by the *whizz, whizz* of a food processor.

What's he up to now? Lauren tries to guess what Nash is concocting. Hummus flecked with seaweed? Beetroot mousse? Cupboards open and shut, and then the oven goes on. Lauren forgets about him, maybe she even drops off, until suddenly she hears the clink of a plate beside her. She opens her eyes.

And there is a meringue, small but perfectly formed, covered with whipped cream and topped with raspberries. Lauren looks through the French doors into the kitchen. Nash is washing up at the sink, a secret smile on his face.

'I thought you didn't cook with eggs?'

'No eggs. It's made with aquafaba.'

'Aquafaba?'

'Chickpea juice.'

'And the cream?'

'Oat.'

'Oh.'

Lauren picks up the fork he has left on the side of the plate and tries a corner of meringue. It's delicious. Gooey and crunchy and extremely light. She wolfs it down.

'There's more,' Nash says, from inside.

'You should put some vegan recipes in your book.'

'Why?'

'I mean, if more men cooked like this...'

'What?' Nash comes back out onto the decking, a tea towel flung over his shoulder. 'If more men cooked like this, what?'

'I don't know. But... it's delicious.'

'Great!' Nash grins. She'd forgotten how perfect his teeth are. His smile is a surprise. 'I'm glad you like it.'

Lauren has a sudden thought. 'What about... *Vegan Recipes for New Age Men*?' she suggests. 'Sounds better than *Falling out of a Tree*.'

'Maybe!' Nash smiles again, but as he picks up her empty plate and carries it away, Lauren can see he is thinking.

* * *

In the kitchen, Nash tries to concentrate on the washing up. Lauren looks beautiful this morning. He peeps out of the window. She is wearing jeans and a brightly coloured blue and turquoise shirt. Her hair is pulled back into a headband which means that most of it is lying obediently still. But a few strands have broken free and are floating in the breeze. Nash suddenly wonders if there are two sides to Lauren. A quiet, conventional side and, underneath, something wilder, waiting to escape. Her eyelids are shut, but then they suddenly open and her green eyes gaze out over the garden.

'Why do you like turquoise?' The question is out before he can stop it.

The green eyes turn in his direction. 'I don't know.'

She's said it defensively, almost irritably. He's gone too far. *Don't be such a creep,* Nash tells himself. 'It's just your house is full of it.' A pause. 'I mean your cottage.'

She laughs then. 'I guess everyone who rents *Fois* asks themselves the same question.' Lauren takes off her headband and her chestnut curls fly away from her face. 'Except I'm not usually here at the same time, so they can't ask me.' Lauren puts her hairband on again. 'Anyway, I don't know.' She is still smiling, but she lies back on the lounger and shuts her eyes again, as if she wants the conversation to finish.

'It's the throat chakra,' Nash says. He can't help himself.

Lauren's eyes open briefly; another flash of green. 'Sorry?'

'The ability to communicate. That's what turquoise stands for.'

'Does it?' Lauren turns over on her side so she is facing away from him.

Nash drains the water out of the washing up bowl and goes to sit in front of his typewriter.

* * *

That evening, Lauren finally gets round to opening the letter that Hamish delivered and discovers that she owes three hundred pounds for electricity for the month of July. Or rather, her squatter does.

She waves the bill in front of Nash's face. 'What the hell have you been doing?'

'I don't know.'

'You must have had the storage heaters on day *and* night.'

'Not all of them.'

'What do you mean, not all of them? They're *night* storage heaters. They're only economical if you use them at night.'

'Oh.'

'You owe me quite a lot of money now. Six weeks rent, and three hundred pounds for the electricity.'

'How about we reach some sort of deal?'

'No deals, Nash. I need the money.'

'What about... what about if I pay you for the electricity now, and then, when my book is out, I'll pay you the six weeks' rent at Christmas rates.'

'What, all six weeks? At five hundred a week? That would be three thousand pounds!'

'A way of saying thank you.'

'That would be great. But how will you pay for the electricity?'

Nash looks startled for a minute, then his face brightens. 'I'll ask Jamie.'

'Jamie who?'

'A friend of mine.'

Nash leaves the room and Lauren hears him talking on his mobile. When he comes back, he is smiling. 'The money will be transferred this evening and in your account tomorrow morning. Is that ok?'

'It's a good start.'

'Yes,' he says. 'Thank you. I really appreciate this, and I won't let you down.'

Nash usually writes at both ends of the day. He finds mornings excellent for ideas, and taps them out excitedly after breakfast. Evenings are more a time for editing. When he returns to his typewriter, he reads what he wrote earlier and adds any bits that are missing. But on the evening of the electricity bill, Nash picks up not his manuscript, but his iPad.

The truth is that Before the Bear Publishing has only offered him an advance of a thousand pounds. If he wants three thousand, he will have to write a bestseller.

Lauren's idea is buzzing round his head. A mixture of vegan cookery and New Age philosophy. If he could get it to work, he could try bigger and better publishers. But he would also have to find an agent. A foodie one. In which case, he will need to contact a few people. He won't bother Jamie again, but he could ask Nigel, or even Delia. She'll know someone.

As he scrolls through his iPad, Nash notices that Lauren is walking down to the shore. She picks her way over the rocks, slowly and carefully, her hands outstretched like a trapeze artist. A few awkward jumps and she is down on the shingle. She is walking quicker now, even though the pebbles must be digging into the soles of her sandals. Then, as soon as she is on the beach, Lauren whips off her sandals, drops them on the muddy sand and takes off. She rushes down the side of the loch, charging along the shoreline, her hair streaming out behind her.

Nash stands up to watch. Lauren doesn't run like a proofreader. She runs like a... like a horse. A flying horse. And her hair is a mane, blowing behind her in the breeze. Nash quickly returns to his typewriter. He has just thought of a new opening for Chapter One.

Have you ever seen a woman run? I mean really run. Flying like the wind beside a stormy sea. Wild running, that's what it looks like. You can live like that. And you can cook like that too.

Nice start. Nash lifts his fingers from the keys, gets up and goes out onto the decking. Lauren is just a dot now; a moving dot, the same size as the seals bobbing in the water. Are they watching her, too?

* * *

When Lauren gets in from the beach, the kitchen is full of steam. On the stove a massive saucepan of water is on the boil. Nash is bending over a pestle and mortar, crushing what looks like walnuts.

'You need to get a grinder,' he says.

'I don't think you're in a position to criticise the kitchen equipment.'

'You're right. It's just the walnuts won't be as...' Nash looks up and smiles. 'Would you... I mean, could I try a new recipe on you?'

'I said no cooking or eating together, remember?'

'This is different. This is an experiment.'

'Should I be afraid?'

'Very!' Nash throws his head back and laughs. Lauren is taken aback by what a nice laugh he has. Warm and infectious. A real belly laugh that she feels startled to have awoken in him.

'I don't want any of that *nouvelle cuisine* nonsense,' she says. 'I'm starving.'

'Entendu!'

'What is it, anyway?'

'Pasta and tomato sauce.' He hesitates. 'I'm afraid I borrowed some of your garlic.'

'But I might need it!' She is lying, of course. She hardly ever cooks.

'Just a few cloves. They'll make all the difference.'

'Can I add them to the bill?'

'Ha, ha!' Nash laughs again. The sound fills the kitchen.

'You're not having any parmesan.'

'No need. I've made vegan.'

'Vegan?'

'Walnuts. You won't taste the difference.'

Lauren goes into the bathroom to wash her feet. The message Nash put on his WhatsApp comes rushing back. ONLY ONE BATHROOM. How ironic that the two of them are now sharing it.

From the kitchen, Lauren can hear the clattering of saucepans, and above it Nash singing 'Hotel California'. It suddenly hits her that he is, in fact, a prisoner here, trapped in a holiday that went wrong. She hadn't considered it from his perspective until now.

The singing stops. 'Ready!'

When Lauren goes back into the kitchen, the table has been covered with a white cloth.

'Where did you get this? Is this a sheet, Nash, because I don't have many and if it gets food on it...'

'Assayez-vous, Madamoiselle!' he interrupts, pulling a chair out.

He flips the knives and forks around her, like a knife thrower at a circus, then brings over a plate of spaghetti covered with a deep red sauce.

'It's pea spaghetti,' he announces proudly.

'Don't spoil it!' Lauren twirls the spaghetti round her fork and opens her mouth.

Nash returns with his own plate and sits down opposite Lauren. 'Don't you like peas?' he asks, his mouth already full.

Lauren doesn't reply. She can't. The sauce is amazing. Smooth and soothing.

'So,' Nash begins.

'Sssh... I need to concentrate.'

'So,' he says again. 'How old were you?'

The question is so out of the blue, Lauren almost chokes. Because she knows what he's asking.

'I mean, when she died.'

'When who died?' She feigns ignorance.

'Your mother.'

'Esther. She was called Esther.'

'Lovely name.' Nash smiles awkwardly.

'I don't want to talk about it.'

'Of course. It's just being here, you know… I'm interested, that's all.' Nash pauses. 'The other morning you used the word *belonged*. You said the walking stick *belonged* to your mother. And I realised then, and I just wondered…'

'I said I don't want to talk about it.'

'Of course. Sorry.'

'Can I get back to the spaghetti now?'

'Sure.'

Lauren takes another forkful. The flavour explodes in her mouth.

'What's the first thing you think of?'

'Sorry?'

'I mean the sauce. What does it make you think of?'

'Can't I just eat it?'

'Of course, but…' Nash puts down his knife and fork. 'How does it make you feel?'

Looked after. The phrase pops into Lauren's head; she bats it away. 'It has a nice taste.'

'Nice? Like what?'

I don't know,' Lauren waves her arm around. 'Warm and comforting.' She hesitates. 'Like a fire on a cold day.'

'Ooh!'

'Now leave me to enjoy my dinner.'

Nash picks up his empty plate and takes it over to the sink. 'Did your mother cook?'

'Nash…'

'I'm so sorry. I won't mention her again.' He drops the

plate in the sink and limps back to the table. 'Can we be friends if I keep my mouth shut?'

Lauren considers. 'Not friends, but not enemies either. We can be housemates.'

'You're on. Housemates till Saturday.'

* * *

Terrific Tomato Sauce

Are you one of those men who occasionally cries? I hope so. Next time you watch a sad film, or read Baudelaire, remember to water the earth. Gaia is parched. She needs your tears!

This dish is guaranteed to make you weep. It needs hundreds of onions, and they must be sharp enough that peeling them makes your eyes water. Peeling the onions is the hard part – this is an easy-peasy sauce recipe that gives boring spaghetti a velvety richness. A dish to impress an unexpected guest!

Serves 2 (Warning – this recipe contains nuts)

Ingredients
4 large or 8 small onions, sliced finely (brown work well, but red are nicer)
5-6 cloves of garlic
2 tins of tomatoes, plum, not chopped – remember to recycle!
250g/9oz spaghetti
A pinch of dried chilli powder
Sea salt and pepper
A handful of walnuts

The secret to this recipe is to sauté the red onions in a frying pan rather than a saucepan. This prevents them from going soggy. Fry them until they are not only softened, but almost burnt around the edges, and have turned a pearly purple, like stained glass.

Halfway through cooking the onions, it's time to add the garlic and put the water on to boil for the spaghetti. Peel the garlic cloves, remove their green centres, chop them finely and stir them into the frying pan with the onions.

When the onions and garlic are ready, add the cans of plum tomatoes, squashing them with a potato masher until they disappear. Notice the lovely thick sauce that envelops a plum tomato, rather than the pale, watery juice you get with chopped ones. Leave everything to simmer for a few minutes. You want the sauce to thicken but not boil away.

Meanwhile, add the spaghetti to the boiling water – a blob of olive oil stops the spaghetti from sticking together.

Next, whizz the sauce with a hand blender. You are looking for red velvet and when you've got it, it's time to season. Check that your guest likes chilli pepper – if they do, a little bit can spice things up nicely – but remember you can't take it out again. Grate some walnuts as a parmesan-replacement topping.

Return to the spaghetti. Fish out a strand with a fork and fling it at the wall behind the stove. If it sticks, it's cooked. If it doesn't – if it falls off behind the back of the stove (!) – wait a few minutes and try again.

Finally, strain the spaghetti, add a glug more oil and serve it covered with the sauce and topped with the grated walnuts. This dish is warm and comforting. Like a fire on a cold day. Perfect for a tête-à-tête!

CHAPTER 4

She must have eaten too much spaghetti, because Lauren has a very bad dream. She is standing in the loch, up to her neck in water. She can't move and it's very cold. She raises an arm and tries to cry for help but her mouth won't open. Patrick swims by. He is doing a front crawl with his head down in the water. When he comes up for air, his face is pointing the other way. Out to sea.

Lauren shakes herself awake and realises it's morning. She tweaks the curtain and looks outside. Everything is covered in a thick white mist. She stumbles along to the kitchen. She wants to be out in it, feel the coolness on her face.

The French windows are slightly stuck with all the moisture in the air and she has to kick them open. From the decking, the only thing visible is the lawn, covered in dew, and beyond it a row of purple willowherb flowers that mark the path down to the beach.

Lauren goes inside again and tiptoes over to the kettle. She doesn't want to wake Nash – she wants to enjoy this on her own. Once she's made her coffee, she takes it back out to the decking. The mist is beginning to lift. The tops of the mountains at the far end of the loch appear and disappear again as the fog billows past like smoke.

Lauren looks out to sea, to where the sun is coming up. The horizon is lost in cloud and the sun is covered in a veil of white that makes it appear like a giant ball of pale, hazy light.

Blinking, Lauren turns back and faces the loch again. Most of the fog has now dispersed, leaving everything glazed with only a thin film of white. Two minutes later, even this has evaporated. The sky is now bright blue and the dark mountains stand out sharply against it. The misty start to the day feels like a secret she was privileged to share.

Hungry for breakfast, Lauren goes back into the kitchen and roots around in the freezer for the croissants she ordered. To her surprise, it says *Vegan* on the packet. She shrugs. Oh well – she can thank Nash for last night's supper. She places two croissants on a baking tray and puts them into the oven.

Ten minutes later, the croissants are ready, but there is no sign of Nash. Lauren eats hers with some marmalade and then, after a moment's hesitation, she eats his as well. She makes another coffee. *He's having a lie in. Enjoy the peace.*

When ten o'clock comes and goes and Nash still doesn't appear, Lauren starts to feel concerned. She walks along the corridor and stands outside his door. 'Nash?'

'Yes?' A weak, strained voice.

'Is everything alright?'

'Sort of.'

'Can I come in?'

'Sure.'

Lauren opens Nash's bedroom door to find him propped up against his pillows. 'Are you ok?'

'Yes. It's just I fell out of bed this morning. Landed on my bruised ribs. It's taking a while for the pain to go down.'

'Oh,' Lauren replies. It feels odd being in Nash's room. Not that it is his room, of course; it's hers. But it feels different in here, and there is a different smell too. Not an unpleasant smell. A hint of cooking – a mix of mint and cumin. Lauren wonders how long it will take the smell to disappear after Nash has gone. 'Can I bring you anything?'

'I think I'm ok.'

'Not even a vegan croissant?'

'You have one of those?' Nash's eyes light up. They are amber, she notices. An unusual colour for eyes.

'Yep. I mean… I didn't mean to buy them—'

'Lovely! And any chance of a Barley Cup?'

Lauren makes a face.

'Please don't make me laugh,' groans Nash. 'My ribs can't take it.'

'Well, seeing as you're mortally injured…'

He smiles gratefully and Lauren goes back to the kitchen. Nash is an eccentric housemate who asks awkward questions and does strange things to her houseplants, and she has nothing whatsoever in common with him, but perhaps it's not so bad having him here. For now. *He's much too hairy for me!* In her head, Lauren practices saying it to Camilla. She pictures the two of them sitting in the kitchen at Jerbil Publishing, having a good laugh about Nash over a cup of Earl Grey. But she won't mention Nash's amber eyes. That would spoil the story.

Lauren's mobile rings as she is taking the croissant out of the oven. She manages to slide it off the baking tray and onto a plate with one hand while she answers the phone.

'I can't take anymore.' Felicity's voice. 'I can't take *her* anymore.'

Lauren can guess who *her* is. 'Do you want me to come back?'

'No. It's no fun in London anyway. Much too busy. Tourists everywhere. I've decided to bring Amelia to you.'

'What!'

'I've hired a car.'

'Hold on, Felicity. There's not enough room here. Not for both of you.'

'I won't be staying. I'm going on to Orkney. I've always wanted to see it.'

'But how do you know Amelia wants to come?'

'I tell you what,' says Felicity, 'I'll put you on to her and you can ask her yourself.'

Lauren stands holding the phone, watching the croissant go cold.

'Hello?'

'Hi, Granny.'

'Have you heard? We're coming up!'

'The thing is, Granny, it's not quite as simple as that. You see, there's someone else here.'

'Patrick?'

'No.'

'Another man?'

'Sort of.'

'Sort of?'

'You see, when I arrived, it turned out that the last person who let the house hadn't left. I mean, he would have left, but he broke his leg, and now… well, now he can't. Not yet. Not until Saturday.' The words come out in a rush, leaving Lauren breathless.

'What's his name?'

'Nash.'

'Nash, like gnash? Like the gnashing of teeth?'

An image of Nash's pearly whites rises unbidden in Lauren's mind. 'No, not that sort of gnash. Nash like the artist.'

'And is he?'

'No.'

'And will he be there when we arrive?'

'Yes.'

'Well, I hope he's respectable.'

Lauren considers Nash's bushy ponytail, his abundant beard, his one lonely flip flop and his plastered leg. 'He's a good cook,' she offers.

'Would he do a roast?'

'I don't think so.' There's no use explaining. Granny doesn't know what vegan means.

There is an altercation in the background and then Felicity is back. 'We'll be with you tomorrow. If I don't kill her first.'

* * *

When Lauren breaks the news to Nash, he seems more intrigued than anything. 'What's she like?' he asks, his mouth full of croissant.

'Like all grandmothers. Annoying. Eccentric. Set in her ways. Lovely.'

'How's she lovely?' As Nash speaks, specks of croissant fly across the bed towards Lauren; other bits catch in his beard.

'Could you?' Lauren gestures to her face, but Nash doesn't get the hint.

'How's she lovely?'

'I don't know. Kind. Concerned. That sort of thing.'

'Are you fond of her?'

'Of course. She's all I've got.' Lauren feels her face flush. *Why am I letting him in on my secrets?* 'I have a boyfriend,' she says, just for the record.

'Do you?'

'I just told you I did.'

'And is *he* lovely?'

'Yes, he is. And he has a lovely flat in Primrose Hill. *We* have,' she adds.

'Lovely boyfriend, lovely flat,' echoes Nash.

'You have croissant shavings in your beard.'

'Something for later!'

'Could you try and act normally while my grandmother's here?'

'Normally?'

'Not hugging the plants.'

'Of course.'

Unconvinced, Lauren goes back to the kitchen. She puts the kettle on but can't bring herself to make another coffee. Instead she stomps around, opening drawers and shutting them again. If she hadn't come up, none of this would have happened. Except Nash would still have been here. Would not knowing have been better or worse? She can't decide.

Lauren checks her food supplies. Given how little her grandmother eats, they will get through the week. Somewhere in the shed, behind a dilapidated lawn mower, is her childhood bike. She can cycle into Dornoch if they run out of food.

Lauren uses the boiled water to fill a hot water bottle and tucks it into the bed in the remaining bedroom to warm the bedding. At least Felicity isn't staying. Even so, the thought of living with both Granny and Nash for a few days fills Lauren with dread.

She decides to have a shower, but when she walks along the corridor to the bathroom, the door is bolted. She goes back to the kitchen, opens and shuts a few more drawers, then goes back and tries the bathroom door again. Still locked. Lauren tries not to think about what might be happening inside. She turns the handle two or three times so Nash knows she's waiting.

'Won't be long!' calls a cheery voice.

'Hurry up!' Lauren rattles the door handle.

'Three minutes!' he calls.

The precision of his prediction makes Lauren flee back to the kitchen. Except he is a *lot* longer than three minutes. When she finally hears the lock slide back, Lauren decides to give the bathroom recovery time.

As she washes up at the sink, there are footsteps in the corridor and the sound of a plate being placed on the kitchen table. 'Thanks for the croissant, Lauren, and sorry for the delay.' A pause. 'I mean in the bathroom.'

Lauren looks round to give Nash a nasty smile and steps

back in surprise. He has shaved his beard off. All of it. The lot. The beard has departed. Flown. Evaporated like the morning mist, revealing a rather startling face.

The beard made Nash look furry and fuzzy around the edges, like a bear. Now it's gone, he looks younger, more angular. His jaw is strong and his cheekbones, previously hidden by sideburn fluff, jut out. He looks like... like what? Like a professional. An accountant, perhaps. Or a stockbroker. Only his long hair gives him away.

'It's bad enough your grandmother discovering that I'm squatting in your house,' he explains. 'I couldn't give her the beard treatment as well.'

'You didn't mind giving *me* the beard treatment!' As Lauren says it, she realises she prefers Nash with a beard.

He shrugs. 'There was no chance of winning you over.'

'Is that what you plan to do? Win her over?'

He smiles then, giving her another flash of his perfect teeth. 'What other choice do I have?' He places one hand over his ribcage and hobbles carefully over to the fridge. 'Time for some baking.'

* * *

Sexy Scones

Scones. If you shut your eyes and say the word, you could almost be at the Ritz. Imagine pot plants and tinkling pianos and waiters approaching with cups of tea. Think of ladies with purple perms. Then think again. I mean, get real. Scones are hip and you will find them at any decent pop festival. Scones are sexy, scones are cool – well, vegan ones are, anyway. And they're not heavy either. They are as light and fluffy as the clouds above Glastonbury. Just follow my recipe and wow your mates.

(Makes tons)

Ingredients
450g/16oz self-raising flour
80g/3oz vegan margarine
200-300ml/7-10 fl oz non-dairy milk (oat works best)
3-4 tbsp sugar (depending on your taste)
Cooking time: 180°C for 10-15 minutes (check for brown
bottoms!)

Baking is a sign of love, and baking with love can
intensify this feeling. I usually bake repeating a mantra.
You can start as you sieve the flour into a mixing bowl.
As you shake the sieve, shake some love into the flour.
Repeat 'I bake with love' a few times as you go.

Next, weigh out some vegan margarine and rub it into
the mixture. If you persevere, the flour will become
sticky and tacky. 'I rub with love' works well here. Now
stir in some sugar, then slowly pour in the milk, a dash
at a time, mixing it in with a knife.

Finished? You should have a mixture that is not too
wet, and not too dry either. A just-right ball of floury
gunk that you can pick up and transfer from the bowl to
a floured tabletop. If you've done things properly, you
will need to wash your hands!

Return to the mixture and squash it down until it looks
the right thickness. Now use a pastry cutter to cut out
some scone shapes. Put them on a greased baking tray
and slide them into a preheated oven.

By the time you've got all that mess off the tabletop, the
scones will be ready. Serve them warm with coconut
spread, or vegan squirty cream and homemade jam.
Warning: these scones are full of love.

CHAPTER 5

The next day dawns bright and sunny. Lauren gets up early, determined to squeeze in a long walk before her hostess duties start. When she goes into the kitchen, Nash is sitting outside on the decking. The cooker is gleaming and the worktops smell suspiciously clean.

'Not bad,' she calls, through the open French windows.

Nash looks round. Once again, Lauren is shocked by the absence of his beard.

'Why only not bad?' he asks.

'You left a teabag in the sink.'

'Teabags are compostable, but you don't have a compost.'

'Surely you could have built one, Nash? After all, you've had plenty of time.'

Lauren opens the freezer and looks for the bag of vegan croissants. Only one left. She slams the freezer shut again. She realises she is not nice enough to cook the last croissant for Nash, and not mean enough to eat it on her own. If only she had bought the normal variety, then she could have scoffed it without feeling guilty.

'There's some scones in the tin,' Nash calls, as if he has read her mind.

'No, thanks.' Lauren silently orders her stomach not to grumble, fills the kettle and goes outside.

It's one of those summer mornings that could have been

lifted straight from a fairy tale. Birds are flying in large arcs around the house. Swallows or house martins, Lauren can never tell the difference, swoop low over her head and then high into the blue sky above.

The tide is out, revealing a sandbank in the shape of a crescent, as if a slice of moon has fallen into the loch. On the sandbank, seals like oversized commas bask in the sun. Their moans and bellows are carried inland by the southerly wind.

'What a noise,' observes Nash. 'It's amazing here,' he adds.

'I think I'll go out,' Lauren says. 'Have a good walk before Granny arrives.'

'Go, go!' Nash replies, giving her an annoying sort of blessing.

The beach seems to have been taken over by birds. Arctic terns run past, leaving tiny footprints in the sand. Eider ducks fly along the shoreline, their long wings like floppy ears. They land on the loch and start making cooing calls, oohing and aahing like gossiping ladies.

Lauren spots two curlews picking their way across the shingly sand. They are instantly recognisable with their long, downward-curving bills, but she sees fewer and fewer of them these days.

She walks past the abandoned jetty where a pair of oystercatchers are nesting. They are furious with her and shriek their disapproval until she's out of sight.

To avoid disturbing the oystercatchers again, Lauren cuts across the dunes and does a long loop home. Marram grasses swish against her legs and she has to watch her step over the uneven, boggy ground. Small Blue butterflies race ahead. Yellow Rockrose flowers light the way. In the distance, a Highland cow calls to its calf.

When Lauren gets back from her walk, the moss-covered gate is open, creaking uneasily on its hinges, and a car has driven in. The boot of the car yawns wide and the front door swings to and fro in the wind. From inside Lauren can hear two voices: one low and mumbling, the other high and insistent.

She steels herself to go through the front door and into the living room, but at the last moment she chickens out and creeps around the back.

Felicity is sitting on the steps of the decking, gulping down a mug of tea and checking her phone.

'Hi!' Felicity smiles. 'You're just in time to save him.' She rolls her eyes and gestures with her head towards the kitchen area.

Granny is standing beside the open French windows. Her suitcase, a pre-war leather one, is parked beside her. Nash has backed himself into a corner between the sink and the cooker.

'Nash?' Granny is shaking her head as if to imply that no one would have such a ridiculous name. 'Nash who?'

Nash seems unsure what his second name is.

'What's your *real* name?' Granny asks.

Nash opens his mouth, closes it again, bows his head and mutters: 'Clifford Adderman.'

Clifford Adderman. Lauren adds this new information to what she already knows. He is, she decides, not a real person at all. He is a shimmering hologram that changes from one moment to another. First a tenant, then a squatter; first a hippy, then a baker; initially bearded, subsequently beardless. Now even his name has changed.

'In that case, I shall call you Clifford,' Granny announces. 'Rather than Nash. Anyway, which room am I in?'

'I'll show you,' says Nash. He picks up the suitcase and hobbles with it along the corridor. Granny follows.

'So who is he?' asks Felicity, not taking her eyes from her phone.

'I've no idea,' Lauren replies. And she means it. She has no real handle on Nash. It's like trying to describe a revolving door.

'And he's...?'

'Staying till Saturday,' Lauren says briskly. 'And then, after his plaster is taken off, he will leave. And I will *never* see him again.'

'That great, hey?'

Felicity, although she would be horrified to realise it, is starting to sound as nosy as Granny. Or perhaps she's just been spending too long in her company.

'Would you like another cup of tea, Felicity, or do you have to head north immediately?'

Felicity laughs and jumps up. Her left foot catches the empty mug and it rolls off the decking onto the lawn. 'Point taken. Anyway, I need to get off. I'm hoping to catch the last ferry.'

'Well, enjoy Orkney.'

'I realise this is rubbish of me,' Felicity says. 'I know you have her all the time. I just can't—'

'I understand. She takes some getting used to these days.'

'Do you think we'll be the same?'

'God help us!'

And then they are both laughing. Felicity gives Lauren a warm, bear-like hug and disappears.

A noise in the kitchen. Nash and Granny are back.

'Would you like a scone with your tea?' Nash is asking.

'I would. And I would like it on the veranda. I know you young people call it the decking, but it used to be the veranda.' Granny steps outside and grins at Lauren. Her eyes are dancing with life. 'You must be livid this Clifford chap has invaded your holiday,' she says. 'And the one person you *really* want isn't here.' She sits down and gazes out over the view. 'Nice teeth, though.'

'Tea's on its way!' calls Nash.

* * *

It's hard to pinpoint when exactly Granny starts approving of the squatter. Probably somewhere between the second and third scone. No obvious outward sign, except her hand starts to sway slightly as it approaches the proffered plate.

'I probably shouldn't,' Amelia says coyly.

'They won't keep till tomorrow,' says Nash.

'Well... if you're sure, Clifford,' smiles Granny, and her hand sways again, as if in ecstasy.

Lauren is relieved that Granny seems to be taking to Nash, but also bemused. She orbits carefully around them.

'Do *you* bake, Amelia?' Nash asks.

Granny's smile becomes more flirtatious. 'Oh no! I mean, not really. Not anymore.'

'So you used to?'

'Well, yes. But nothing exotic.'

'You can't beat good old-fashioned British baking,' Nash smiles. If buttering up grannies was a game show, Nash would win hundreds of prizes.

'Clifford's vegan,' Lauren says mischievously.

Nash's head whizzes round and he gives Lauren a look. Probably because she's called him Clifford, but maybe also because she's landed him in it.

'Ve... Gun?' Granny looks confused.

'I don't eat animals or their products,' explains her baker.

Granny chews thoughtfully. 'Tastes alright,' she says. Another flirtatious smile: 'What's for supper?'

* * *

With a flourish Lauren finds positively annoying, Nash serves up new potatoes which have been boiled, then fried in herbs, garlic and sea salt; mushrooms – which Lauren saw him pick, so who knew if they were safe or not – cooked in a creamy garlic sauce (oat milk); and homemade sausages, vegan style. Granny has seconds.

After a pudding of wild raspberries from the hedgerows and homemade pear sorbet, Granny pushes back her chair and reclines in a satisfied stupor.

Lauren starts to pick up the plates, but Nash won't have it.

'I'm on duty tonight,' he smiles. He limps over to the sink and slides the plates into the soapy water.

'I could get used to this!'

'Not too bad, was it?'

'If the mushrooms don't kill us, I'll give it an eight.'

'Only an eight?'

'It would have been a nine if you hadn't stolen my pears.'

'They were going soft.'

'It's still theft.'

Nash lifts a plate out of the water, rinses it, slots it into the draining board and then leans on the edge of the sink.

'Is your leg hurting?'

'Not hurting exactly. It gets heavy at night.'

'Thanks for cooking, Clifford.'

'Please don't call me that.'

'Why?'

'I like Nash better.' He turns from the sink and looks at Lauren. His amber eyes gleam in the gloom of the kitchen; she turns away.

* * *

That night, lying in bed, it occurs to Lauren that Nash is in fact two people. And she finds herself googling Clifford Adderman on her phone. Nothing much comes up, then she sees a post on Twitter written by someone called Hannah Strawlight. *I will never forgive Clifford Adderman*, the post says. *For he has broken my heart*. For some bizarre reason – Lauren has no idea why – her own heart starts thumping. She quickly clicks off Twitter. 'Bastard,' she whispers.

* * *

The next morning, Lauren wakes to a new sound.

'Relax your muscles!' The voice, which belongs to Nash,

is coming from the garden. Lauren looks out of the window.

Granny and the resident hippy are standing on the decking, moving their arms like slow windmills. Nash is wearing a T-shirt and baggy tracksuit bottoms which hide his plastered leg. Granny is wearing linen pyjamas and a towelling dressing gown tied at the waist. She looks quite the martial arts expert.

'Deep breaths,' Nash is saying. 'In and out.' A pause, and then: 'You are beautiful!'

As if in response, Granny's arms spin faster.

Lauren pads along the corridor into the kitchen and peers through the French windows.

'And relax!' Nash is calling.

The spinning has stopped. Nash is standing just in front of Granny, moving his arms in and out like a bird preparing to take flight. Granny is watching and copying. Her chest is rising and falling in time with her instructor.

'You are wonderful,' Nash tells her.

Lauren's eyes fill with tears.

'Come on, Lauren.' Granny notices Lauren watching and beckons her to join them.

Now her cover is blown, it's too tempting not to join in. In fact, it's irresistible. Lauren steps through the open French window onto the wooden deck.

'Pick up the wave,' says Nash. 'Let it wash over you.' He puts his hands together, then brings his arms up and over his face.

The wood feels cool on the soles of Lauren's feet and the air is full of the sweet smell of morning. Lauren watches Nash's moves, then copies them, imagining she is washing herself with air. It feels hypnotic.

'Push away the stress!' calls Nash. He lifts his arms and pushes them out to his sides, hands raised like a policeman stopping traffic. His eyes are still shut but his nostrils start opening and expanding in a way that makes Lauren want to giggle. And maybe that's why she can't push away the stress; because she is giggling too much. Granny seems to be managing it, extending her arms up and outwards, her flat palms pressing against the resistant air.

'You need to relax, Lauren.' Nash's voice. 'Learn to let go.'

'I can't!' And then Lauren topples over.

Nash opens his eyes and Granny's arms come down again. She looks at Lauren reproachfully.

'That's enough for today,' says Nash.

'Enough what?' Lauren feels like a disruptive child at the back of the class.

'Qi gong,' says Nash. 'Granny's a natural.'

'Hands off!' Lauren laughs. 'She's my granny.'

And yet it's sweet, Nash calling her *Granny*. Patrick always refers to her as Amelia. And he doesn't call her anything to her face, because they have hardly met. Once, perhaps, at someone's wedding. Whose? Lauren's mind clouds over.

A green tiger beetle bumps into her leg, then lands on the decking beside her. Lauren stoops down to examine its iridescent back, dotted with yellow spots. As if it senses her enormous shadow overhead, the beetle flies a few feet with a buzzing sound, then scuttles away on its long legs.

The sun is shining on the lawn, turning it almost yellow with light. Lauren bends under the handrail of the decking and jumps down onto the wet grass. It feels lovely under her bare feet. As she pads around, Lauren notices how the garden has changed. The beech hedge that borders the lawn has grown higher and quite spindly in places. Some of the topmost twigs are enveloped in lichen, as if they are wearing green, furry hand warmers. Lauren never sees lichen in London. It needs an environment with almost no pollution at all. Up here lichen grows everywhere, coating the tops of walls and climbing the trunks and branches of trees.

'Coffee, Lauren?'

'If you're making it.'

Lauren pads around a bit more, then swings herself back onto the decking and sits in the sun, peeling pieces of wet grass off the bottom of her feet. A kitchen towel flies through the French windows towards her.

'Thanks!'

'Is that the hand towel?' asks Granny. 'Because that's not what it's for.'

Lauren glances through the kitchen window. Nash gives her a conspiratorial wink.

* * *

Marvellous Meringues

This chapter is mostly a hymn to the humble, honest, modest chickpea. A most unassuming legume, the colour of earwax and yet the magician behind dishes like humous and falafel. There is no waste in this recipe. Not only is the can recyclable, but the liquid that the chickpeas come in can be reused as well. It can be whisked into peaks as thick and glutinous as egg whites, and these peaks can become meringues as delicious as any you've ever tasted.

Nash pauses and lifts his fingers off the keys. He gets up and hobbles over to the kitchen window. On the decking, Lauren is sitting playing cards with her grandmother. She is wearing a light blue dress with a pale yellow cardigan, which contrasts with her long chestnut hair.

Nash stands and watches. He thinks about his first night, when he felt Lauren's aura in the house and couldn't decide if she was a communicator or not. In fact, she is both. She is a lighthouse: one minute closed and dark, the next open and illuminating. She is unguarded then secretive; she gives then she holds back.

Nash notices a bee buzzing on the window ledge beside him and lets it out of the window. It flies straight over to the ladies and Granny tries to knock it out of the way.

'Don't, Granny!' cries Lauren. 'I love bees!'

Nash adds this new information to his list. Loves bees. Can't relax. A proofreader that runs like a horse. Then he returns to the typewriter.

Let's get back to the chickpeas and, more importantly, their juice. Bean water. It sounds very pedestrian, which is perhaps why it is known to chefs as 'aquafaba', which sounds much more glamorous! Here is how to turn aquafaba into meringues.

Ingredients
1 can of chickpeas
125g/4oz caster sugar
½ tsp cream of tartar or ½ tsp lemon juice

Preheat the oven to 100°C. Drain the can of chickpeas into a large bowl and keep the liquid. That's the aquafaba. Add the cream of tartar or lemon to it and whisk. Slowly, slowly is the secret here. Allow the starch in the beans to create the magic. The aquafaba will take twice as long as egg whites to thicken, but that's ok. You are standing at the forefront of experimental cuisine – and you have all the time in the world.

Watch as the liquid slowly turns to thick, glossy paint, then paint with a whirlpool at its centre. Allow your thoughts to swirl down the whirlpool and disappear. This is cooking at its most Zen. You are chilled. Do not consider how many minutes you have been doing this, or the impact it will have on your electricity bill. Instead, drift away.

Once the mixture begins to form peaks, add the caster sugar one spoon at a time, whisking in between. Tip the last of the sugar in, letting it fall into the bowl like sprinkling snow. Keep whisking until the mixture begins to rise into snowy mountains, then spoon it onto a greased baking tray and place into the preheated oven.

Bake for about an hour, or until the meringue is hard to the touch. Allow to cool and then serve with whipped oat milk, or sweetened, condensed coconut milk, and raspberries.

A sound of laughter from the decking. Nash stands up again and wanders back to the open window. Lauren and Granny. Thick as thieves. Nash can almost feel their intimacy, and half of him wants to interrupt it, wade in, enjoy their company. But three's a crowd. Besides, the other half of him wants to protect their closeness, respect it, let them float off together like a bubble on a breeze. He feels a sweetness tinged with sadness that catches in his throat.

* * *

It's hard to remember her mother's face. Lauren has photos, of course, but they are fading now. The albums that house them are fading too, and the glue that holds the pictures in place doesn't work anymore. When Lauren turns the pages, most of the photos fall out onto the carpet.

But she can remember doing things with her mother. Watching dolphins in Cromarty Bay, feeling the weight of the binoculars around her neck and her mother's hand on her shoulder. Standing together on Oxford Street and gazing at the Christmas display in Selfridges, mittened hand in mittened hand. In Lauren's memory, she and Esther are always looking in the same direction, rather than at each other.

Perhaps people don't look at each other much. Patrick doesn't, anyway. He looks at her in bed, when the light is off, his dark eyes scanning her face. But at breakfast the next morning, he looks at the newspaper.

It suits her, the not looking. So Lauren feels a bit unnerved when she feels Nash watching her. It's not creepy. It's not even intense. But it's thoughtful in a way that makes her worry.

'What?' Lauren turns suddenly and catches him.

'Just checking you're not cheating.'

'Takes a cheat to know a cheat.'

'Indeed.' Nash turns back to his typewriter, moving from the window to the kitchen table with an ungainly lurch on his good leg.

'Will it be a relief to get the plaster off?'

'Yes and no.' A pause. 'I'll miss not being here.'

'And *Fois* will miss you too,' Lauren smiles. 'Even though you're a scrounger.'

'I told you I was going to pay Christmas rates!' Nash sounds tense and Granny looks up from her cards.

'It was just a joke, Nash,' says Lauren. Then, 'If you want to exercise your good leg, we could have a walk later.'

It's an olive branch, and Nash seizes it with both hands. 'Lovely! I need to get some writing done, but maybe tonight? After supper?'

'I'll stay here,' says Granny. She triumphantly fans out her cards. 'And that's Rummy.'

Granny smiles, and more photos pop into Lauren's mind. She and her mother flying a kite at Sandwood Bay, leaning back into the wind. Her mother dragging a Christmas tree out of a car. Granny and Lauren with their arms around the neck of a Shetland pony.

There are lots of albums, but most they never look at. Some things are best forgotten.

* * *

Lauren's great-aunt was called Muriel. She was a doctor who decided to retire early, move to Loch Fleet and convert an old byre into a home. Muriel loved her job but her second love was birds, and she planned to live out the rest of her days cataloguing the local population. Of course, life never works like that, and the first winter she came up to Loch Fleet, Muriel died of a heart attack. As she had no children, she bequeathed the cottage to Lauren's mother, Esther.

Sometimes Lauren wonders if this was a good idea. If Esther hadn't been left *Fois*, maybe she would have gone to university or college or got a job. Perhaps she would still be alive, working for a shipping company, say, or a travel agent's, and living in a suburban house with a tidy lawn and a washing line. *What if, what if.* Thoughts like this made Lauren's brain ache.

When Esther died, the cottage passed to Lauren, along with a strange collection of things. Old-fashioned things that no one needed these days, but that Lauren can't bring herself to get rid of.

There is a butter churn by the back door. A dark wooden barrel with a long wooden handle, it stands gathering dust behind the wellies. Then there's an enormous sunhat in the shape of a triangle that looks like it comes from the Tropics and which provides the same amount of shade as a small shed.

But there is one heirloom that Lauren really likes. A gramophone has pride of place on the coffee table in the living room. It looks old, although how old she's never bothered to find out. The wooden box is engraved and includes a small picture of a dog gazing into a brass trumpet.

After her triumph at cards, Granny wanders in to the sitting area, flicks through the records, selects one and winds up the gramophone.

> *Ye banks and braes o' bonnie Doon*
> *How can ye bloom sae fresh and fair?*

The song floods the house, making the saucepans rattle.

From her lounger on the decking, Lauren can see that Nash isn't welcoming the distraction of the music. His typing increases in intensity and the carriage return pings more frequently.

Perhaps Granny senses this too, because when the record is finished, she puts it on again. And again.

Eventually Nash gives up, gets to his feet and limps over to join her.

Lauren stays outside, but she cranes her neck around the French window. Nash sits down on the floor beside the records, his plastered leg stretched out in front of him, the other tucked under him, and reads the different record labels in turn. After a few minutes, he slides a record out of its paper sleeve and shows it to Granny.

'This,' he says, 'is one of my favourites!'

'You weren't even born,' says Granny scornfully, as she holds the record up to the light and squints at the title. 'But it's a good choice,' she adds and, with the terrible sound of a needle scraping across vinyl, she pulls the old record off the gramophone and puts the new one on.

A few seconds of scratchy silence while the needle finds its groove, then a different song starts up.

A-roving, a-roving
Since roving's been my ru-i-n

At that moment, the mobile in Lauren's pocket starts to buzz. It's Patrick. Lauren usually gets a butterfly feeling when Patrick phones, but this time his call flusters her. There's such a racket going on. She nudges the French window shut with her foot and goes to the far end of the decking to try and escape from the music.

'Hello?'

'Hi, Lauren. How's it going in the frozen north?'

'Well…' Lauren fills Patrick in as quickly as she can. She knows he never has long to chat when he's at work. Also, he can lose concentration quite easily and she's learnt to be concise.

'So he's been there six weeks without paying?'

'Not quite six. Five and a half.'

There is a commotion behind the French windows, and then they open, and Nash and Granny appear doing a strange sort of dance – a cross between a waltz and a foxtrot. Nash's plastered leg gives him a lopsided gait, and the two of them look like a couple of demented penguins.

Lauren backs off to the end of the decking.

'I can't hear you now,' Patrick says.

'Sorry.' Lauren shoos the penguins back inside and edges closer to the house.

'What's that noise?'

'Just some music.'

The penguins reappear. One of them, the female, begins hooting with laughter. '*A-roving, a-roving,*' she croons.

'It's not past the yard arm,' Patrick observes. 'Why is your grandmother singing?'

'*I'll go no more a-roving with you, fair maid.*' Nash's voice now, quite close to the phone as he whizzes Granny round the decking for a final spin.

'Is that the squatter…?'

'It's the record,' Lauren lies.

But then the singing stops, and there is the sound of whooping and clapping and Granny cries: 'Bravo! What a dancer!'

'I'm coming up,' says Patrick.

'Coming up! But why?'

'I thought I was invited?'

'Oh, you are – I mean, you were – but that was before…'

'Before what?'

'It's just… it's a bit chaotic here.'

'In what sense?'

'Well, Nash is a little eccentric, and… and it seems to bring out Granny's… hold on, I thought you had your AGM?'

'Cancelled.'

'Oh.'

'If I start driving tonight, I'll be with you tomorrow afternoon.'

'Right.'

'So I'll see you soon.' And Patrick is gone.

* * *

In order to fill long, boring car journeys, Granny and Lauren used to play a game. They planned imaginary dinner parties and invited people who didn't have the slightest hope of getting on with each other. Mostly the guests were people they knew, but they could fill in with famous personalities if there was an empty place. In real life, Granny never had dinner parties, and this made the game even more enjoyable. They thought up menus too, making sure that every course would have something to offend one of the diners. The aim was to create at best a tense atmosphere and at worst an almighty row, and they used to giggle at the thought of potential outbursts.

Now, the game appears to have come true. Not a nightmare dinner party – no, worse than that – a nightmare sleepover. Probably two sleepovers, because Patrick will want to stay at least a couple of days.

Lauren staggers inside and collapses at the kitchen table. 'Patrick's coming up.'

'Lovely,' Nash smiles. 'Isn't it?'

'It depends,' Lauren replies.

'We'll be good, won't we?' Nash looks at Granny.

'Always!' grins Granny.

'Is he sleeping in your room or mine?' asks Nash.

* * *

Despite their jokes, Nash and Granny take Patrick's arrival seriously. Granny gets the vacuum cleaner out and spends a long time hoovering up things that make a terrible crunching noise as they disappear into the hoover bag. Nash talks about making a Vegan Wellington, which he promises will taste just like a Beef Wellington only nicer, and says he will forage for some bilberries.

'Why bilberries?' Lauren follows him into the front garden to ask.

'Because there are no cranberries here and my recipe needs cranberries.'

Nash stomps along the road beside the hedgerow. His leg seems to have got stronger and he hasn't mentioned his ribs recently. In a strange kind of way, Lauren is glad everything is healing. It would feel like a bad omen for her letting business if Nash didn't recover from his stay.

Nash swivels round on his plastered leg and smiles. 'I hope your lover's arrival won't scupper our walk tonight?'

Lauren had forgotten about the walk, and if she had remembered she would have cancelled it. But Nash's use of *lover* confuses her.

'Sure. I mean, no, it won't scupper it.' Lauren shrugs her shoulders and disappears inside.

* * *

In fact, it is Granny who almost scuppers the walk. At supper time, she announces that she would like to come too.

'Marvellous,' beams Nash. 'It will do you good to stretch your legs. Besides, there's nothing on telly apart from *Antiques Roadshow*.'

'*Antiques Roadshow*? Perhaps I'll stay behind.'

'Just starting,' says Nash brightly. 'I could put it on for you?'

'Thank you, Clifford.'

Nash fiddles with the television, then disappears into the scullery and reappears leaning on Esther's walking stick. 'No running, Lauren! Take pity on the wounded!'

They walk through the back garden and onto the scrubland that leads to the loch.

'I thought *Antiques Roadshow* was on on a Sunday?' Lauren asks as soon as they are out of earshot.

'The wonders of iPlayer,' smiles Nash.

'That's devious! But, to be honest, we wouldn't have got far with her in tow.'

And suddenly Lauren is glad. Glad that she has a chance to stroll along the lochside in the evening sunshine. Not for the first time, she thinks to herself that Nash isn't all bad. Cheeky, yes – outrageously cheeky in overstaying his welcome by more than a month – but he has been sweet to her grandmother.

'So,' Nash begins, as he propels himself forward, using the walking stick to do a strange sort of hop, skip and jump over the shingle. 'Why proofreading?'

'Why not?'

'But why? I mean, give me a reason.'

'Nash, if this is some sort of careers interview, I think I'll go back and watch telly.'

'It's not. I guess I just want to know you better.'

'And I could ask the same question of you? Why the qi gong and the reiki and the flip flops?'

'I asked first.'

Ahead of them, a flock of oystercatchers is standing by the water. Lauren wonders how close they can get before the birds rise as one and fly over the loch.

'Well?'

'Precision.'

'What?'

'Proofreading. It involves precision. That's why I like my job.'

'Right.' Nash sounds unconvinced.

And I feel in control. But Lauren keeps that to herself. Saying it will suggest she is out of control. 'And the publisher is great. It's a lovely place to work.'

'Which publisher?'

Oh no. I'm not giving that away. 'Before the Bear.'

'But that's *my* publisher...' and then Nash laughs. 'You're teasing.' He gives Lauren a little push, which is unfair as she can't push him back, not without him falling on the slippery stones.

'You write, I proofread,' Lauren says, hoping that will be the end of it.

Nash stops for a second and closes his eyes. Lauren takes the opportunity to check on the oystercatchers. They are still there, but there is an imperceptible tension within the group.

'I see you working with people,' says Nash, keeping his eyes shut.

'I prefer words.'

The oystercatchers take off, zooming across the loch, white wings flapping like prayer flags.

'So, what about you?' Lauren says, keen to deflect the conversation away from herself. 'Why the New Age lifestyle?'

Nash stops again. But instead of closing his eyes this time, he looks away, following the oystercatchers over to the other side of the loch. 'I haven't always been vegan,' he says eventually.

It feels like a clue, though a strange, cryptic one.

'What do you mean?'

'I mean I'm too avant-garde for my own good.' A rueful smile.

The sand squelches uneasily under Lauren's feet. There is something Nash is not telling her. No, more than something. A whole load of things.

'Let's stop asking questions.' He grins at Lauren, but there is a pleading look in his eyes.

They walk on silently, but not uncompanionably, until they reach the ruined jetty. Lauren loves the way the old, bleached pillars of wood stick out of the water, criss-crossing into the air like the ribcage of a whale.

'And Patrick?' asks Nash.

'What?'

'I mean, why Patrick?'

'So the careers advice has changed to marriage counselling?'

Nash swings round to face her, his stick flailing helplessly in the air.

'Are you married?'

'No.'

'Oh.' He thinks for a moment. 'Would you like to be?'

'It seems that there is one rule for you, Nash, and another for me. I thought we just agreed—'

'We did.'

They wander on. The tide starts to go out, funnelling its way back into the sea. Lauren loves this constant filling and emptying of the loch, like lungs breathing in and out.

'Just one more question...' Nash begins.

'I grant you one more question, Mr Adderman. Choose carefully.'

'I mean, look at it.' Nash waves his stick in an enormous arc, like a wizard casting a spell on the landscape.

'You mean, why do I live in London, and not here?'

Nash nods his head.

'I really don't know.' It's the first time Lauren has admitted this to anyone. There are lots of reasons for staying in London, Patrick being the most obvious. But why does she live amongst the smog and traffic, when...?

'Your grandmother would come,' muses Nash. 'So, if Patrick—'

'Nash...'

'You're right. I shouldn't be asking.'

'I might add this interrogation to the bill.'

'Do.' A pause. 'Although perhaps I could get something deducted for entertaining Granny?'

'I'll give you a thousand off if you give her a game of Monopoly.'

'Monopoly!' groans Nash. 'I'll do it for two.'

They have reached the head of the loch. The sand is firmer here. They are back on solid ground again. Where the loch finishes, the mountain begins. The sun is setting behind the summit, throwing its steep flanks into shadow. Lauren imagines deer high up, trooping across the bracken, enjoying their last graze before nightfall.

A seal swims past, carried by the current. It notices them and sniffs the air. Then it pokes its head and neck right out of the water and stares. A flick of its dark, shiny body, and it's gone.

'Shall we go back?'

Instead of answering, Nash grabs Lauren's arm. He is gazing at the sky above the mountain. Lauren turns to look in the same direction.

There is a flash of light and something drops out of the sky onto the mountain top. Something long and gold, like a necklace, but blazingly bright and falling fast. It must be a ray of sun, one of the last of the day. And yet it feels more solid than that. The ray, the necklace, whatever it is, pauses briefly on the summit, creating a halo of light. Then it slowly slithers down the side of the hill like a golden snake. Down, down it slides and into the loch. For a second, it forms a line of light across the water; then it disappears.

'Have you ever seen that before?' Nash whispers.

Lauren shakes her head.

'Something has happened. Something tremendous.'

'You can put it in your book.'

'You don't realise. Everything has changed.'

'I don't see how.'

'Well… not everything. You and me.'

He is still holding her arm. Lauren tries to pull away, but he holds her tighter.

'I have a boyfriend, Nash.'

'It's not about that. It's about…' Nash pauses, lost for words, waving his stick around as if he is trying to include the loch and the sky.

'We'll get over it,' Lauren says, wondering what she means.

'But that's the trouble. We *won't*.'

There is something about the way Nash says it, with the emphasis on the *won't*, that frightens Lauren. She turns away from him and starts hurrying up the beach, back to the cottage. She can hear Nash lumbering up behind, slow and ponderous. She hears the click of his stick and his plastered foot sliding on the wet stones. He isn't chasing her, she knows that, and yet she increases her pace. When she reaches the garden she glances back. He isn't even following now. He has stopped at the edge of the shingle and is looking up the loch. And yet Lauren finds herself sprinting through the garden towards the house. She opens the French windows, rushes through the kitchen and down the corridor.

Safely in her bedroom, Lauren dives under the duvet and reaches for her phone, charging on the bedside table. It feels like a relief to hold it in her hand. She scrolls through her contacts. Patrick is filed away under ICE – In Case of Emergency. And it is. She presses the call button. The phone rings out. *Come on, come on.* The call goes to voicemail, and then she hears Patrick's message. *Sorry, I'm unable to answer right now. Please try later.* Lauren clicks off, but she keeps hold of the phone in her hand, and when she hears Nash limping down the corridor towards his room, she says 'I can't wait to see you, Patrick.' And she forces a smile into her voice and says it again. 'I can't wait to see you.' Then she adds, 'Ciao,' even though neither of them speak Italian. An oystercatcher flies past the window with a screech.

CHAPTER 6

One of the many advantages of driving gloves is that Patrick doesn't have to touch anything in a service station, not with his bare hands anyway. Door handles, card readers, toilet locks – Patrick feels them all through the leather, but he avoids real contact. And for this protection he feels particularly grateful. It's the middle of the day and the place is teeming with people. And not the sort of people Patrick is used to. Stopping at a service station, he realises, is like a game of roulette. You never know what you're going to get until you park up and go in, and by then it's too late.

Ever since he left London, Patrick has been looking for somewhere to stop with the perfect combination of a Waitrose and a Starbucks. It's only here, in the middle of Lancashire, that he's found a service station with the two together, and on his side of the road.

Safely installed in the coffee shop and stirring his cinnamon latte, Patrick asks himself why he is making the long journey north and realises it's a combination of things. Firstly, as soon as Lauren had left, Patrick realised that he also needed a holiday. Secondly, and this is slightly embarrassing considering he and Lauren have been together for three years, he has hardly ever been to *Fois*, and he wonders now if that has ever bothered her. Thirdly, and perhaps most importantly, there appears to be another man staying there.

Who is this *Nash*? And is he interested in Lauren? It was hard to tell from the phone call, although it was obvious he was getting on well with Lauren's grandmother. Patrick realises, a little late in the day, that he should have shown more interest in Amelia. It wouldn't have taken much. The odd bottle of plonk, sent via Lauren on one of her visits. A poinsettia at Christmas. Now he will have to double his efforts. He picks up a box of champagne truffles, inspects the price tag and puts it back. He's bound to stop again, and further north everything will be cheaper.

* * *

When she hears Patrick's car pull up beside the cottage, Lauren jumps up from the sofa.

Nash struggles up from his chair and looks out of the window to inspect the new arrival. 'Driving gloves,' he mutters.

As she runs out of the front entrance and down the path, Lauren realises that Nash has put his finger on the only thing she doesn't like about Patrick.

'Hello!' she cries, rushing towards the driver's door.

She sees the sleeve of Patrick's jacket through the window, she sees his gloves being pulled off and placed on the seat, and then Patrick is getting out onto the grassy parking spot. 'You made it!' Lauren flies over the daisies towards him.

'Hello.' A soft smile, and then he gives her a squeeze.

'I can't tell you...' Lauren laughs as she hugs him back. Her long hair flies around in the wind; it's in her mouth, then his. 'I can't tell you how pleased I am.' She remembers how horrified she was at the thought of him coming up, and how that horror has turned to relief. And she doesn't let herself think about why. 'Come and meet the others.'

The scene in the living room looks strangely staged.

Granny is sitting upright in the armchair with the *Radio Times* unopened on her lap. Nash is crouched behind his typewriter.

'This is Patrick. Patrick Mounder.' Lauren's voice sounds as if she has just jumped onto a train seconds before it was due to leave the station. 'Patrick, this is Nash Adderman, and you've met Granny already.'

Granny looks up from her magazine and her eyes flicker across Patrick's face. 'Only once.' And then, as if even she realises this sounds a bit rude, 'Good journey?'

'Fine, thank you. Long.' Patrick's eyes meet Granny's. 'Too long.' He smiles; she doesn't. He is the first to look away.

'You made it!' beams Nash, getting to his feet and hobbling forward to shake Patrick's hand.

Lauren silently compares the two men. Nash is tall, with long mousy hair and those angular cheeks she still hasn't got used to. Patrick is smaller and more delicate. Dark, curly hair, expensively cut; a boyish face with large, bright eyes that add a seriousness and a sexiness. There's no doubt about it: Patrick is sexy, and Nash is messy. *Sexy; messy. Sexy; messy.* She repeats it to herself like a mantra. *Sexy; messy. Sexy mess; messy sex.*

'You must be gagging for a cuppa!' says Nash.

Lauren expects Patrick to wince at Nash's language, but he smiles. 'Please.'

'Put the kettle on, Clifford,' Granny says.

A wave of confusion crosses Patrick's face.

'Granny calls Nash Clifford,' Lauren explains.

'Why?'

'It's his real name,' Granny says, her gaze fixed on her *Radio Times*.

'Oh.' Patrick seems bemused.

'I'm a fraud!' laughs Nash.

'Right.' Patrick looks bewildered now.

'But a great chef,' says Granny.

'How was the journey?' asks Nash.

'Long,' replies Patrick, in an *I just said it was long* kind of way.

'I can't imagine driving that far,' Nash grins. 'But she's worth it.'

Patrick gives Nash a look that says *What do you mean?*

'She is,' Granny chimes in and smiles at Nash.

'Let's take your bag to our room,' Lauren says. She grabs Patrick's hand, the one Nash has just shaken, and leads him away.

'Don't forget to come back for your tea!' Nash calls after them.

They don't go back. They lie on the bed, fully clothed, and hold each other. The warmth of Patrick's chest; the feel of him; the smell of his aftershave; it's comforting and familiar. But it's hard to forget that Nash and Granny are just along the corridor. She hears Nash guffaw at something Granny says. His loud belly laugh floats down the corridor towards them.

'He's strange,' Patrick whispers.

'Thank God you're here,' she whispers back. As she says it, Lauren sees the golden necklace dropping down the mountain. She remembers Nash's hand on her arm; the intense colour of his eyes. She blinks the vision away.

When they go back through to the sitting room, they find a commotion going on.

Around a dozen bluebottles have crawled out of the window frame and are looking for an exit. Granny is brandishing a fly swatter and Nash is acting as chief fly negotiator.

'Couldn't we release them into the wild?' he is asking.

'They'll only come in again,' Granny replies.

'But they all have souls,' Nash reminds the executioner. 'Every single one of them.'

'I don't care!' cries Granny.

'They do!'

'The circle of life?' Patrick smirks.

'The wheel of karma,' replies Nash.

'Let me at them!' shrieks Granny, accidentally bashing Nash in her attempts to get past him to the insects.

Patrick disappears and comes back with a rusty-looking can of fly spray. 'I found this in the scullery,' he says. 'Should do the job.'

'No!' moans Nash, covering his eyes.

The can has a picture of a fly in its final stages of agony. Even Granny looks doubtful.

'Stand back!' Patrick orders. He aims the can at the bluebottles.

The nozzle fizzes, produces a strange sort of foam and then suddenly the air is full of a vile-smelling spray.

The flies react immediately, zooming chaotically in all directions before falling onto the windowsill with a crash. Some of them spin helplessly, their legs waving in the air.

Granny finishes them off with the flyswatter. She looks quite upset.

'A plague on both your houses,' mutters Nash and limps outside.

* * *

Although she has never seen Patrick eat vegetarian, Lauren realises that she was, until this point, hoping Nash would cook them all supper. This is no longer possible. He has gone off in a huff and is sitting on the decking, eating the bilberries that were meant for the Vegan Wellington.

Lauren finds a shop-bought quiche in the fridge, sticks it in the oven and throws a salad together. Patrick, who seems happier now that Nash is out of the way, opens a bottle of wine and chats amiably to Granny.

Over supper the chat turns to property. Patrick asks Granny all sorts of questions about her house in Croydon.

Does she like living there? What's the street like? Is the garden too much for her? Does she talk to the neighbours?

'You must come round,' says Granny, her mouth full of quiche.

'I would love to,' replies Patrick. A pause while he helps himself to salad, and then: 'Have you ever had the place valued?'

'Conveyancing is Patrick's speciality,' Lauren says quickly, in case Granny takes it the wrong way.

'I have no plans to sell,' says Granny.

'Of course not,' smiles Patrick. He quickly finishes his salad, gets up from the table and starts to wash up. Granny sits and watches. Then she goes to bed.

'Let's go for a walk,' Lauren says. 'It's a lovely evening.'

They sidestep Nash, who is still sulking on the decking, and go down the steps onto the grass.

Lauren can't help feeling the irony of the situation. She's always hoping Patrick will come up to Scotland with her, and now here he is. It's like one of those dreams where everything should be going well but it isn't. Instead there is a massive spanner in the works – two, in fact.

Lauren tosses her head as if to shake Nash and Granny away and takes off her sandals.

The grass is damp and squeaky under her feet. She tries to concentrate on the feeling it gives her: the sensation of drinking a cool, green drink.

'Let's go down to the beach.' Patrick slips his arm around her and together they duck beneath the boughs of the apple tree. They negotiate the rough ground, the stones and then the shingle. The tide is coming in.

'Oh, blast! I'm wearing the wrong shoes,' Patrick says, when he sees the soggy-looking sand.

'Oh.' Lauren looks at his suede desert boots. 'Couldn't you take them off?'

'I'd rather not.'

'Well, we'll have to go back then.' Lauren can barely conceal her disappointment. She desperately needs to revisit the loch with Patrick. She wants to rewrite yesterday's strange experience, or, even better, experience it again, and this time with the right person. She glances down the loch. The sky above the mountain looks a boring pale colour, slightly cloudy in places. Absolutely no sign of magic.

Coming back over the rough ground towards the garden, Patrick lets go of Lauren's arm and starts batting the air around him. 'Midges,' he explains.

Lauren looks up to see a mass of tiny insects has gathered above Patrick. A small, dark cloud which is magnetised to the space above his head. Forwards or backwards, left or right, whichever way he moves, the cloud moves too.

'Are they bothering you as well?' Patrick asks.

'Not much.' Lauren silently wills the midges to bite her instead. But they continue to follow Patrick everywhere, like a group of ardent disciples shadowing their teacher.

'Why are they only after me?' moans Patrick, scratching his cheek.

Lauren suspects it might be the Thick and Strong hair pomade that Patrick uses occasionally, but she's not going to say that out loud, not with Nash within earshot. 'I eat a lot of Marmite,' she replies. 'They absolutely hate the smell of it.'

'It'll take more than Marmite,' says Patrick. As they bend under the apple tree, the midges hover lower and closer. 'Ow!' He bats one away from his face.

'Ho, ho!' Nash's voice from the decking.

'I suppose you think these are the bluebottles reincarnated?' scowls Patrick.

'Too soon!' laughs Nash. 'Although God help you when they do. No, this is karmic retribution, pure and simple.'

'Was it karmic retribution when you fell out of the tree?' Lauren asks.

Nash considers the question, then smiles. 'If it was, it was good karma. It meant…'

'You could stay here for nothing?'

'For now,' replies Nash quickly. 'Only for now.'

* * *

Lauren must have her own karmic debt to pay, because she sees Nash again much later that night. She needs the loo and, of course, when she gets there the door is locked. And, of course, it's Nash. Who else would it be? Lauren can hear him peeing in a way that Granny would never manage.

Patrick goes down on one knee to pee, like a man getting knighted. *The polite way*, he tells her. Nash, she can tell from the noise, is peeing standing up, as if from a great height. After the chain has flushed, the tap runs for what seems like a decade.

Lauren decides to go back to bed and return when Nash has finished, but then the door opens suddenly, and out comes Nash. To her relief, he is wearing pyjamas.

'Hello,' he says.

She steps to one side to let him pass but doesn't reply.

'Ok?' he asks.

'Of course.'

Nash hesitates. 'Good.' He moves off slowly down the corridor.

Lauren leaps into the bathroom and bolts the door. It's only when she's safely back in bed that she realises no one can kneel with a leg in plaster.

* * *

Now he has met Lauren outside the toilet, Nash feels wide awake. What is it about her that makes him feel so completely alive?

She is not the kind of woman he usually goes for. Beautiful, of course, but a carnivore. With no interest in New Age thinking. A proofreader, for goodness' sake. And yet.

He pictures Lauren kicking off her sandals and running along the loch; her whole body electrified. He considers the way her green eyes close when she's eating; how she picks up a glass of water with both hands and gulps it down like a child would. The way her long hair flops over her face and how she tucks it behind her left ear, which is as small and pretty as a shell. She is funny, with a wit that surprises him on occasions. She is sharp, too, especially with him, but underneath he senses softness, like the dewy lawn she walked across this evening.

Nash groans. He is wasting his time. Lauren has a boyfriend. Not one he would have chosen, but a boyfriend nevertheless, and currently manifesting physically just along the corridor. Nash has never been a relationship wrecker, which means the only solution is to either start to dislike Lauren, or start to like Patrick.

As it seems unlikely he could ever get to like Patrick, perhaps it would be easier to dislike Lauren. Or at least feel nothing for her. Nash imagines her with greasy hair and spots. Nope, not working. He pictures her old, with wrinkles and chin hairs. Hopeless.

Nash tries the other tack. There must be something to appreciate about Patrick. He examines Lauren's boyfriend close up and then from a distance, but there doesn't seem to be a single redeeming feature. Even Patrick's car, a souped-up Jaguar, has leather seats. Added to this, he is a fly murderer. And how can a man so liberal with fly spray love a woman who runs like a race horse? He can't.

This realisation hits Nash hard, right in the chest. He sits up and holds his rib cage, then he realises the pain isn't coming from his ribs. It's deeper than that.

Nash gazes round the bedroom, trying to keep his mind off, well, things. Perhaps a novel? There's one in his rucksack.

Holding his side, he bends down to pull his rucksack out from under the bed. It's been there so long it has got jammed in, and he has to yank hard on the straps to free it. When it finally comes loose, it brings other stuff with it. A broken lamp, a pair of slippers and a book. No, not a book – a photo album. Nash picks it up to put it back under the bed, but as he does, half the photos tumble out onto the carpet.

This is awkward. And none of his business. Nash starts to shove the photos back in the album. He tries not to look at the pictures, but then a larger photo catches his eye.

A young woman is sitting by a camp fire. She is strumming a guitar, eyes half-closed. Her hair is the colour of Lauren's, but longer, reaching down to her waist. Around her lounge other people, men mostly, but there are women too, sitting cross-legged, or lying in the grass. Everyone is smoking something and there is a languid feeling in the air. As if they have been around the fire for a long time.

Behind the woman is an apple tree that looks just like the one outside in the garden. A smaller version, but with the same slight twist in the trunk and the same lower branches.

So this is Esther. Quite a beauty, but with a rather dazed expression.

And now Nash can't stop looking, glancing at each picture before sliding it back inside the album.

It's like flicking through one of those animation books when you turn the pages and the story comes to life. He sees Esther pregnant, her bump steadily growing, and then suddenly there is a baby in her arms. And the baby grows slowly into a toddler, and then a tomboy. *Lauren*, he realises with a lurch. Lauren grinning in a swimsuit and flippers. Lauren flying past on a sledge. A lovely snap of her hanging upside down in the apple tree; another of her holding a ram's skull by the horns and sticking her tongue out.

There are other pictures, too. Often out of focus. Pictures of people laughing and gesticulating, eyes half-closed. And always the same heavy smoke, making its way around the party like a snake.

The last picture is different. Another group photo and, as usual, Esther is in the centre. But Lauren is in it, too. She is standing at the edge of the picture, as if she is keeping a distance between herself and the others. She's older now. Six maybe, or seven. There is a sullen expression on her face and she looks like she would rather be anywhere else.

The men in the picture all look like hippies. Unkempt guys with long ponytails and bushy beards. And, to his horror, Nash realises that they look like he does. Or rather he looks like them. He doesn't have the beard at the moment, but his hair would have fitted right in. And he doesn't just look the same; he *is* the same. No job, no money and no fixed abode. Not to mention the fact that he has stayed at *Fois* for six weeks without paying. Lauren's less-than-warm attitude towards him and his lifestyle was starting to make sense. What a shock it must have been for her to arrive and find him squatting in the house. In her eyes, he would have looked like just another drifter. Another long-haired layabout.

CHAPTER 7

Lauren wakes to rain pattering on the window. Oh no. Patrick hates rain. She wriggles down to the end of the bed, lifts the curtain and looks through the rain-streaked glass. The sky is grey and heavy, and the clouds seem to be pushing down onto the hills on the other side of the loch as if they want to squash them flat. The grass between the cottage and the beach is an astonishing green. Emerald green. But Patrick won't appreciate the grass; he'll look up at the sky. For now, he is lying on his back, eyes closed, lost to the world. Perhaps by the time he wakes up the weather will have cleared. Lauren slips out of bed, pulls on jeans and a jumper, and sneaks out.

In the kitchen, Granny and Nash are playing a Top Trumps game of baking disasters.

'I once burned a batch of brandy snaps so badly I never got them off the baking tray,' Granny is saying. 'After that, I had to bake around them.'

'That's nothing,' Nash replies, 'I did the same with jam tarts and set the oven on fire.'

'Ha!' Granny cries.

Nash looks up as Lauren approaches the kettle. 'Do you bake, Lauren?'

Lauren gives a sarcastic smirk. 'Of course.'

'She'd rather swim with jellyfish!' Granny shrieks.

'Would I?' Lauren makes herself a cup of coffee and carries it carefully to the sofa at the other end of the room. She needs as much distance as possible between herself and Nash.

The two bakers burble on, heads together, exchanging notes. Occasionally there is a little laugh. Lauren lets her mind go blank, floating away down the soaking garden and onto the beach where she knows the sand will be dark with rain.

There is a creak in the corridor and Patrick appears in the open doorway. His legs are bare and a few chest hairs peek out of the top of his Paisley dressing-gown. Patrick never wears pyjamas. Lauren wonders what Granny thinks about this and glances over at her, but Granny hasn't noticed, hasn't even looked round.

'Morning.' Patrick addresses the kitchen with a smile.

'Hey!' Nash replies politely. Granny still doesn't turn. Lauren realises that Granny is playing games with both men. With Nash it's the baking disaster game, fun and competitive. With Patrick it's the game of not being the slightest bit interested, which is more aggressive. It feels as if they are all back at school and Granny is picking teams, and she has picked Nash and she is not going to pick Patrick.

Perhaps Patrick feels it too, because he stays away from the kitchen and comes to sit beside Lauren on the sofa. Right beside her – closer than usual.

'Do you fancy going out for lunch?' he says, stroking her hair. 'I mean, the weather's terrible, and you said there's a nice café in Dornoch.'

'There are several. I'll take you to my favourite.' As she speaks, Lauren moves away slightly. She likes Patrick touching her, it's just...

'You look lovely this morning,' says Patrick, stroking her cheek this time. 'It suits you being here.'

Lauren feels Nash watching, motionless at the kitchen table, like a heron standing at the water's edge. She knows there is yet another game being played: a *this is my girlfriend* game. And Patrick is winning it.

* * *

Lauren wills the morning to go faster than it does. Everyone hangs around the living room area. Nash types sporadically at the dining table; Granny flicks through the *Radio Times*; Patrick scrolls through his phone. Lauren jumps up and down, asking people if they would like a coffee and what they want in it and then proceeds to give the wrong drinks to the wrong people. Patrick ends up with a sugary concoction with oat milk, which should have been for Granny except she doesn't take oat milk either, and Granny ends up with one of Nash's teabags. *Heaven Sent*, it says on the packet.

At ten o'clock, Lauren phones the café and books a table for one o'clock. She says *a table for two* twice, just so there can be absolutely no doubt.

Hamish arrives with a letter for Nash and comes inside for a scone. He chats to Granny, slaps Nash on the back and shakes Patrick's hand.

'So there's post up here too?' asks Patrick. He looks astonished.

'Aye, even in the back of beyond!' laughs Hamish, taking Patrick's question as a joke rather than an insult. 'We have doctors and everything. No need for tribal medicine!' And he laughs again.

It's a relief to have someone jolly around, and Lauren keeps Hamish much too long, asking questions about people she barely remembers. Eventually he manages to escape and they are on their own again.

Outside the rain streams down. It's colder out than in and the windows quickly steam up, adding to the feeling of claustrophobia inside. It feels like the start of a dark thriller set during a holiday where everyone falls out and ends up eating each other.

Finally Lauren is in Patrick's car and driving up the hill. The rain has stopped and the puddles reflect the spindly birch trees that line the road, bending them in half.

When they park in Dornoch and get out of the car, the air feels clean and fresh, as if everything has been washed. It's the first time Lauren has been into town this trip. It's a joy to see the old sandstone houses clustered around the ancient cathedral with its gravestones leaning every which way.

Dornoch has everything. It is one of those old-fashioned towns that is so compact and self-sufficient no one needs to go anywhere else. People do, of course – they go to big supermarkets in Inverness. But there is still the lovely feeling that you could live here and never need to leave. There's a supermarket in Dornoch too; they're everywhere these days, but there's also a chemist-cum-post office where you can buy things like bed socks and Yardley talc. There's a library that is cool in summer and cosy in winter, a hardware and grocery store, a wool shop, friendly cafés and a treasure of a bookshop.

On the way to the café, Lauren notices a crowd clustered at the front of the supermarket, looking at the door of the cathedral. A piper in full Highland dress emerges, playing the pipes, followed by a bride and groom.

Normally, Lauren would join the crowd and watch the couple getting covered in confetti, but today it feels awkward, as if she has somehow arranged the wedding for Patrick's benefit. An enormous hint that shouts *Marry me!* They've never talked about marriage, it's strictly a no-go area; an unspoken taboo.

'Come on, or we'll be late,' Lauren says, pushing her way through the crowd, hurrying away from the sound of bagpipes as if the wedding is just an annoying distraction. She can sense Patrick right behind her and she realises that he is even keener to get away.

They turn a corner and there is the café, its windows lit up by warm lights. They go in and find their table.

'Good afternoon!' A smiling waitress delivers their menus.

'I'm going to have something really meaty,' Lauren says. 'I've felt too guilty to cook flesh with a vegan staying.'

'There's a vegan special on the board,' says the waitress.

'No thank you!' cries Patrick. 'I'm not a vegan.' He looks at Lauren. 'Lucky we didn't bring Clifford, our resident chef.'

As the waitress disappears, the man at the next table turns to them with a questioning face.

'Clifford?' He echoes. 'I'm sorry to eavesdrop on your conversation, but not Clifford Adderman?'

'Yes,' says Lauren.

'I didn't know he was vegan. Of course, it might be a different Clifford Adderman, but it's an unusual name.'

'You know him?'

'Only by reputation.'

'Reputation?'

But the man's lunch has arrived. He turns to greet a battered haddock, and doesn't turn back again.

Only by reputation. The words ring in Lauren's ears. She remembers the tweet by Hannah Strawlight. *Clifford Adderman has broken my heart.*

It's such a relief to discover what a cad Nash is. Lauren suddenly feels ravenous and orders just about everything on the menu. Cullen skink for starters and then a burger. And she has dessert, too: a chocolate pudding with clotted cream.

After lunch, Lauren and Patrick stretch their legs on Dornoch beach. They walk along the caramel-coloured sand until a squall of rain drives them back to the car. Then they sit in the car park with the windows down and watch the waves. It's obvious that neither of them wants to go back to the cottage. If only they weren't on holiday here. Anywhere but here.

* * *

When they finally return home, there is a serious game of Monopoly going on. It looks like Granny has cleaned up in the West End. The blues of Park Lane and Mayfair and the greens of Oxford Street, Bond Street and Regent Street are covered with hotels. Granny is sitting with a cruel smile on her face, waiting for Nash to land on something expensive.

Nash throws a double and, like a Monopoly-loving Tigger, comes bouncing along the reds and the yellows, avoids Fenchurch station with a 'Phew!' which suggests it is also part of Granny's assets, and lands on the Water Works.

'It's mine!' he cries. 'I'm safe!'

Lauren glances at Nash's property portfolio. He has been a cheapskate, investing only in Utilities and Old Kent Road.

'You have to roll again,' orders Granny.

'I can hardly bear to!' Nash groans, from the safety of the Water Works.

'I'll get you this time,' she grins.

But Nash rolls a double one and ends up in jail.

'Go to jail, go directly to jail! Do not pass Go!' shrieks Granny.

With a face full of despair, Nash drags his counter back over the yellows, the reds, the oranges and the pinks, until he is behind bars.

'I'll be in here for ages, now,' he moans. 'And no two hundred pounds for passing go. You'll win for sure.'

'Isn't that a Get Out of Jail Free card?' Patrick bends down and points to where a bit of white card is sticking out from under Nash's end of the board.

'Oh.' Nash grins sheepishly and hesitantly pulls the card out.

It occurs to Lauren then that Nash doesn't want to win; that he wants Granny to win, and that Patrick is trying to put a stop to that. 'I need to have a lie down,' she says. 'All that lunch…' She glances at Patrick. 'Are you coming?'

But Patrick has sat down on a chair and is surveying the board like a self-appointed referee.

Nash tosses the Get Out of Jail Free card into the middle of the board and slides out of prison. 'Your go, Granny,' he smiles sweetly.

Lauren feels annoyed with Patrick for making Nash look good. 'Please come and lie down with me, Patrick.' She is practically begging him now.

'I don't want Nash cheating.' And Lauren knows that what Patrick means is that he doesn't want Granny winning. *But why not?* she silently screams. *How bad would that be?*

Lauren stomps off to the bedroom, but she doesn't get into bed. She stands at the window, drumming her fingers on the sill. How can Patrick be so childish? Or Nash? Or Granny for that matter?

Eventually, she hears a cheer go up. 'I always win!' Granny's voice.

Patrick comes into the bedroom and lies down. 'If there's one thing I can't stand it's people who don't play properly,' he mutters with his face in the pillow. And then, 'I thought you were having a sleep?'

'Actually, I think I'll have another stroll.'

'Ok.'

Lauren slips out into the weather. It's still raining over the loch, but inland it looks brighter. She turns away from the water and climbs the road that leads up the hill towards Dornoch. As she walks, the rain stops and a watery sun appears. The sheep in the fields grow big, blobby shadows and their fleeces catch the light.

The sun gets stronger, so Lauren keeps going. She walks to the top of the hill where the road turns into a wood. Mature trees overhang the route and a canopy of leaves weaves patterns on the tarmac. On one side of the road there is a banking covered with ferns, and splashes of sun shine through the dark greenery. It's beautiful and calming. She wants to keep walking. Forever.

* * *

When Lauren eventually gets back to the cottage, her three visitors are sitting in the living room with cups of tea.

'Imagine it,' Nash is saying. 'A tree full of beauty. Verdant in the summer heat. And through its branches, a glimpse of sea. A thin, sparkling line of water.' He smiles round at his audience.

Lauren realises Nash is trying out a line of his book and automatically starts to put in the commas.

'Back to the story,' says Granny.

'The tree was calling to me. So I started to climb. I wanted to get as far up in the branches as possible.' Nash glances at Lauren. 'Not to damage the tree in any way, just to...'

'Commune?' she offers.

'Yes!' Nash grins at her. 'To commune with the tree. And I did. I straddled an enormous branch, leaned my head back against the bark and stretched my arms out to touch the leaves—'

'And then?' interrupts Granny.

'I fell. Right to the bottom.'

'Ha!' Granny cries.

'Did you know that you'd broken something straight away?' asks Patrick. As the lawyer in the group, Patrick is trying to establish the facts.

'No. I think I must have lost consciousness for a bit, and then, when I came round there was this enormous dog...'

'Dog!'

'Hound. An enormous hound sniffing at my shorts.'

'Urgh,' Lauren says. She can't help it.

'Why?' asks Patrick.

'I had a bar of chocolate in my pocket.' Nash glances at Lauren again, 'Vegan, of course.'

'I don't care...' Lauren starts to say, but Nash is racing on with his story.

'I think the dog, I mean hound, could smell it.'

'Dogs will eat anything,' said Patrick.

'Yes, but I was worried it would take a bite out of my...'

'Ha!' shrieks Granny.

'So I tried to get up and, well, I couldn't. And the hound was sniffling and snuffling and I knew I was in real trouble.' Nash pauses to grin at his audience.

'Were you in pain by now?' Patrick switches back to a legal tone. Lauren wonders if Nash is going to sue. The tree's owner, perhaps, or even the tree itself. Surely not.

'I could feel a dull pain in my leg, but my ribs were on fire.'

'You broke your ribs?'

'Bruised them.' Nash pauses and then: 'The doctor told me bruised ribs can be more painful than a break.'

'Really?' Granny loves a good health story.

'Intercostal muscle strain,' says Nash, as if he has suddenly remembered.

'So, what then?' asks Patrick. He has his professional hat firmly in place now.

'I took one look at the hound and I screamed. I mean—'

'Bellowed?' Lauren suggests.

Nash gives her a grateful smile.

'Why do you keep looking at Lauren?' says Patrick.

'I don't.'

'You do.'

The room goes silent. In the kitchen, the fridge-freezer starts to hum.

'Then what happened?' asks Granny eventually.

'The dog's owner found me and called the emergency services.'

It's probably the punchline, but no one seems to notice.

'Is it raining again?' Granny asks.

'Nope,' Lauren replies. Why do people say *nope* instead of *no*? Perhaps to make *no* sound less abrupt. Which makes it a good word to use when one is not sure what else to say. Useful at times of great awkwardness.

'Who's cooking tonight?' Granny makes another attempt at conversation.

'I'll do it,' offers Patrick.

'No, I will,' says Nash. 'I'll make us all Vegan Wellington, like I promised.'

'You always have to muscle in,' says Patrick irritably. He gets up and disappears into the kitchen. A minute later he comes back with a packet of rice and waves it at the rival chef. 'I'll cook rice and lamb chops.'

Nash seems unsure how to take this. 'Sure,' he shrugs.

'And you,' continues Patrick, tossing the bag of rice from one hand to the other, 'you can just eat the rice.'

'Which is why Vegan Wellington would be better,' replies Nash. 'Because we could all enjoy it.'

'Will you just shut up.' And Patrick lobs the bag of rice at Nash. But it soars across the room harder and faster than it should, hitting Nash squarely in the chest.

'Oh!' The sound is out of Lauren before she can stop it.

Nash bends double, but only momentarily, like a man who knows he has been shot but then realises it's a rubber bullet. 'It's ok,' he gasps. 'I'm fine.'

'Sorry,' says Patrick, looking awkward. 'I forgot.'

'No worries,' replies Nash. And he hobbles out of the room.

'I forgot he'd hurt his ribs.' Patrick addresses his words to no one in particular.

'Well, you've got rid of him anyway,' says Granny.

Now Patrick looks stricken. He walks down the corridor and stands outside Nash's bedroom door.

'Sorry, mate, I forgot you'd hurt your ribs.'

Lauren has never heard Patrick say 'mate' before. She listens out for a response from Nash, but there is no reply.

Patrick walks back into the kitchen area, picks up a pan and takes it over to the sink to fill it with water. Granny stays in her chair, but she stares at Lauren. Lauren can feel

Granny's eyes boring into her like lasers. Lauren refuses to meet her gaze. Instead, she looks out at the rain.

* * *

The Best Rice in the World

In this recipe, I'm going to tell you how to make the very best rice. Not that cooking is supposed to be competitive; cooking is all about nurturing and sharing. But it's good to know that in terms of flavour and texture, your rice would eclipse anyone else's.

Nash pauses to rub his ribs, then continues.

Some blokes just put rice in a pan and boil it, producing something either hard or sticky, under- or overcooked. But not you, my friend – or at least not anymore!

Compulsory ingredients
Rice! 1 cup of rice equals 2 portions (The size of the cup equals the size of people's appetites.) I like Basmati best.
1-2 tbsp vegan marg/spread

Voluntary ingredients
1 chopped onion (sautéed)
1 chopped fennel (lightly fried)
1 clove garlic (sautéed)
A handful of sultanas
A handful of almonds (toasted)
1 bay leaf

Wash the rice. If you have the time, soak it in cold, salted water for about 30 minutes. Otherwise put it in a sieve and give it a good dousing under the tap. Drain.

Melt 1 or 2 tablespoons of vegan marg/spread in a thick-bottomed pan. Stir in the rice until the marg is absorbed (2 mins). Pour in water or vegan stock to just above the level of the rice. Add a little salt (no need if you're using a stock cube or my Simmering Stock Pot recipe). Tossing in a bay leaf is also nice.

Cover and cook slowly, stirring occasionally, adding more water or stock if needed, until the rice is al dente – or soft if preferred – and the liquid absorbed.

You can enjoy your rice 'naked' or add some of the voluntary ingredients. (My advice would be EITHER the onion OR the fennel, not both!) Stir them into the cooked rice and serve. You will be amazed how a simple dish can become a melt-in-the-mouth sensation.

CHAPTER 8

Lauren goes to bed straight after supper with a terrible headache. She lies in the dark, listening to Patrick and Granny whispering in the corridor; then Granny and Nash. Eventually everyone goes to bed. But Lauren's head is still thumping and she can't settle. She gets up and wanders along the corridor to the kitchen. To her surprise, she finds Nash.

He is standing at the sink, looking out at the garden. The moon is bright and it's just possible to make out the branches of the apple tree. When she comes in, his head snaps round. 'Lauren. Are you alright?'

'Yes.' Lauren staggers over to the living area and lies down on the sofa.

'I couldn't sleep,' Nash explains. He falls silent but Lauren can hear a noise in his throat as if words are fighting with each other.

'You shouldn't...' Nash begins, but then he stops himself, '...eat meat,' he finishes lamely.

Lauren doesn't ask what he was going to say, but she knows it wasn't that.

Nash flops down on the chair opposite her but then he jumps up again. 'He doesn't care!' He almost shouts it.

Lauren sits up as if she has been electrocuted. 'Who doesn't?'

'Patrick.'

'Patrick?'

'And he never will.'

Lauren feels her headache fly away, to be replaced by pure white anger. Bile rises in her throat; she swallows it down. 'You come here, you overstay your welcome, you use much too much electricity, you intrude on my holiday, and then you think you have the right to comment on my relationship!'

'I would have kept quiet if it had been anyone else. But how can a man who wears driving gloves, who doesn't even want to touch the steering wheel, how can a man like that be intimate with other people? He can't. He's detached from everyone. Even you.'

'And I suppose you would never treat a girl badly? Never break a heart, never build up a bad reputation?'

'I don't know what you mean.'

'I guess now you're *Nash*, you can leave the misdeeds of Clifford Adderman behind you. Well, Patrick doesn't need to change his name. He's a decent, upstanding lawyer and he has driven all the way from London to see me. So he *does* care. How dare you suggest otherwise?'

Lauren knows she needs to get away before Nash has a chance to fight back. His words have battered her. She feels like the jetty on the shore, still standing but half-wrecked by the sea. If he has another go, she might topple. Lauren stands up, but Nash stands too and takes her arm.

'Patrick's the type who will never love anyone. Not properly, anyway. Believe me, you're worth so much more...'

'How do you know?' Lauren is almost shouting now.

'Because you're not who you think you are. Not who you appear to be. You're hiding your...' Nash seems momentarily lost for words. 'I've seen you run, Lauren. I've seen the real you.'

'The real me?' Lauren fills her voice with sarcasm. It seems the safest emotion right now.

'You're not a quiet proofreader, Lauren. You're wilder than that. And you're still a tomboy at heart.' Nash stops, as if he realises what he has given away.

'How do you know I was a tomboy?'

'I'm sorry. I didn't mean to look…'

'Look at what?' But Lauren has guessed.

'I didn't mean to. They fell out from under the bed.'

'How dare you!' Lauren takes comfort in her anger. It means she can forget about what Nash has just said about Patrick. And about her. She can ignore it all and concentrate on Nash's crimes.

'So it wasn't enough to squat. You had to spy, too. You had to probe into my past, look at my photographs. Is nothing safe from you?'

'I'm so sorry,' Nash says. 'It was an accident.'

'An accident! And are you happy now you know everything?'

'No, I'm not.' Nash looks distraught. 'It must have been so difficult for you. Stuck here with Esther and…'

'I was eight.'

'What?'

'The other day you asked me, so now I'm telling you. When my mother died, I was only eight.'

'I'm so sorry…'

'About what? Sorry you've stirred everything up for me with your snooping and questions and opinions I never asked for?'

'I'm so sorry,' he says again.

'Do me a favour, Nash. When you get back to London, leave me alone. Completely. Don't ever contact me again.'

Lauren hurries out of the room before Nash can reply. She goes into the bedroom and crawls under the duvet. Patrick is lying facing the wall. She needs him to take her in his arms.

'Patrick?' she whispers. 'I feel dreadful.' Tears are leaking out of her eyes.

'Poor you,' Patrick says, sleepily. But he doesn't turn around. Instead he reaches out a hand behind him, gives Lauren a pat and goes back to sleep.

* * *

Why did he say it? Why can't he ever keep quiet? Nash has never felt so wretched. Lauren will hate him now, if she didn't already. Nash blunders around his bedroom, knocking into the furniture. *Don't break anything. You've done enough damage.*

He has never felt anything like this before. This pain that is sweeping through him. He thinks about the pain he felt in his leg when he fell from the tree. It was nothing compared to this. And it's all his own doing.

He could have left quietly, without falling out with Lauren. So why did he fall out with her? What possessed him? Now she never wants to hear from him again. How could he have managed things so badly?

He has always been much too honest. When will he learn that people don't want to hear the truth? Anyway, he only told Lauren half the truth. He told her that Patrick didn't love her, but he didn't tell her that *he* did. Or at least that he could, that he would, given half the chance. But maybe that was good, because Lauren wouldn't want to hear that either. Not from a squatting hippy with no prospects.

'Anyway,' Nash mutters to himself, as he rolls his clothes into an enormous ball and chucks them into his rucksack, 'You can't love someone you hardly know.' And yet it feels like he does know Lauren, inside and out. As if she has somehow slipped inside him.

When Nash first arrived at Loch Fleet, before he fell out of the tree, he spent hours wandering in the dunes, swishing through the long grasses, trying to remember the names of the wildflowers and butterflies, and he always came home covered in burrs from the thistles and bushes. Now it feels as if Lauren is a burr, one that has caught in his heart. And there's nothing he can do about it. All he can do is leave quietly, go home and work like mad until he can pay the rent he owes her. And forget anything else. *You have absolutely no chance*, he tells himself. *Not now.*

What a nightmare. And tomorrow he has his long-awaited hospital appointment in Inverness. He needs to catch the first bus from Dornoch to get there on time. He was hoping to cadge a lift into town with Patrick. Now that's impossible.

Still, there's always Hamish. Saturday is the postie's day off and he works as a taxi driver at weekends. Nash finds his mobile and sends Hamish a text.

I KNOW IT'S LATE NOTICE BUT ANY CHANCE OF A LIFT TO THE 8.30 BUS? COMMERCIAL OF COURSE. NASH

Once the text is sent, Nash continues to pack. He needs to be careful not to forget anything. Lauren won't take kindly to finding he's left something behind.

A text from Hamish pings in. NO WORRIES NASH. I'LL BE OVER FOR 8. H.

Nash turns off his phone.

* * *

Lauren lies awake, trying not to think. Along the corridor she can hear Nash packing. Despite their row, despite everything Nash said, she can't help wondering how he will get to Dornoch tomorrow.

Forget him, she tells herself. *Let him miss his bus.* Lauren turns over and puts her head under the pillow. Outside the window, the sea is rumbling. There must be some sort of storm away from the coast because it's much louder than usual. She pictures the waves in the North Sea grinding and churning, coming closer to the shore.

CHAPTER 9

Nash shuts the front door quietly behind him and drags his rucksack down the path towards Hamish's silver taxi. Hamish takes Nash's rucksack and opens the boot. Nash limps round to the front passenger door.

'Hey, thanks for this, mate. Sorry you've had an early start.'

'Nae bother. It's great to have a change from the post.'

'Cool motor. Passat?'

'One of the old models, before the shape got rubbish.'

They pull away and head up the hill. Nash doesn't look back at the loch; doesn't need to. He knows it by heart.

'You always lived here, Hamish?'

'Aye.'

'Did you… did you know Lauren?'

'You mean when she was wee?' It's a windy day and a gust buffets the undercarriage. 'A bit, aye. We were at the primary together. She lived here then. With her mum.'

'What was she like? Lauren, I mean.'

'A wee thing. But bold. A tree-climbing type. She loved running, too.' A pause. 'She didn't stay long.'

'Oh?'

'She stopped coming to school.' Hamish hesitates and then, 'I think it was a bit chaotic at home.'

'Right.'

'You ken how folk talk…' Hamish goes quiet.

'So?' Nash asks eventually.

'Her grandmother came and took Lauren and her mum back to London.'

'Both of them?'

'Aye. *Fois* lay empty for ages. I used to pass it on my bike.'

'And Lauren was how old then? I mean, when they went back.'

'It's too early for questions!'

'Sorry. You don't have to…'

'Let's think. Six, seven maybe.'

'And her mother…'

'You'll need to ask Lauren that yerself.'

'She doesn't want to talk about it.'

'Well then.'

They fall silent. Nash counts the birch trees that border the road, leaning over in the gale. *She hates me; she hates me not; she hates me.*

'So who's the other fella?' Hamish asks. 'Saw him arrive in that Jag of his.' He laughs. 'Posties don't miss much!'

'Patrick? That's her boyfriend.'

'But I thought…'

'No.'

They have reached Dornoch. The town is still sleeping but there are a couple of backpackers at the bus stop.

'What do I owe you, Hamish?'

'Get away. After all that baking…'

'Really, I want to pay.'

'Awa' with you.' Hamish jumps out, pulls Nash's rucksack onto the pavement and gets back into the taxi. 'Watch the wind doesn't take your door.'

Nash clambers out. He shuts his door carefully and lumbers round to Hamish's side of the car. 'Please let me…' Nash says.

Hamish opens his window a crack. 'I tell you what. Next time you're up, you can pay me in cake.' And then he's gone.

* * *

The squall that whipped up the sea last night has come inland. The willowherb is leaning right over and the apple tree creaks uneasily. Lauren struggles onto the decking and into the wind, pushing against its force. She stretches her arms out like a kite to see if she can take off.

It's not a day for walking, but something draws Lauren to the beach. She needs a blast by the shore to blow away yesterday's upset.

The tide is on the turn. The waves are still coming in, over and over, but growing weaker every time. And in between the waves, there is a pull that flattens everything, that stretches the water backwards, as if the land has started to slope and the sea is sliding away. It's a moment of change and instability.

The old jetty has disappeared, flattened by the storm. Just a few wooden posts lying in a heap like felled tree trunks. The oystercatchers who nest on the end of the jetty are circling round and round where it used to be, their cries full of dismay.

When Lauren returns to the cottage, Granny and Patrick are sitting at the dining table eating toast.

'He's gone,' says Patrick. 'Left with what's-his-name.'

'Oh,' says Lauren. *He's gone.* She waits for relief to come pouring in. But it doesn't.

'Got a lift with the postman,' Patrick continues.

'Hamish,' says Granny. 'I saw them go.' And then: 'He left this.' Granny waves a note in the air.

'Oh,' says Lauren again. Her mouth feels dry.

'IOU 3K' reads Granny out loud. 'What's a K?' Granny asks Patrick, her eyes dancing with mischief.

'It means the hippy is under the illusion that he will be able to pay his debt of three thousand pounds.'

'When?' asks Granny.

'Never,' says Patrick. A pause. 'I think we should go back to London later today.' He looks at Lauren. 'It will be easier for you than taking the plane on Sunday. It'll be door-to-door if I drive.'

'What about Felicity? She'll be back from Orkney tomorrow.'

'She's got a car, hasn't she?'

'I guess so,' Lauren replies. 'It's just she was going to take Granny home.'

The thought of driving six hundred miles with Granny and Patrick fills Lauren with dread. She can see that Patrick is swithering too.

No,' he says eventually. 'I think we should get going today. Amelia, I would be happy to drive you home. Although perhaps not all the way to Croydon. There are plenty of minicabs from Primrose Hill...'

'Thank God for Patrick,' says Granny, with an irony that makes Lauren wince.

* * *

Amelia has seen many things in her life. Many depressing things. She can even remember the Blitz. She was only a child when it happened, but the collapsed buildings, the smoking houses, the children climbing on mounds of rubble looking for broken toys, it is all fixed in her mind. And there have been other low moments. The death of Esther so young, with Lauren still just a tot.

And now this moment, the moment of leaving Loch Fleet, will have to be added to the depressing column. Having commandeered the front seat of Patrick's Jaguar, Amelia leans her head back on the headrest and tries to work out why.

There is nothing wrong with the man beside her. He's not bad looking, if you like smaller men. And he is polite enough, although sometimes the politeness seems false, as if he *tolerates* rather than *appreciates* the older generation. He looks after Lauren, but only up to a point. Compliments her too, but not enough for Amelia's liking.

So what it boils down to is that the London lawyer has nothing to condemn him, but nothing to recommend him either.

Amelia realises that her stay at *Fois* was more enjoyable before the arrival of Patrick. And the cooking was much better.

Patrick had cooked with... with what? Duty, perhaps. Whereas Clifford had cooked with... And then it hits her like a bolt from the blue. *Love.*

'Everything alright, Amelia?' asks Patrick, keeping his eyes on the wheel.

'Yes.'

But it is not alright. The 'L' word is out of its box and dancing along the road in front of them. Amelia glances over her shoulder to where Lauren is snoozing in the back seat. She wonders if she has seen it too.

* * *

Lauren sits with her eyes shut, pretending to sleep, but she can tell that Granny is turning round and giving her little glances.

Lauren can guess what Granny's thinking. If Granny knew about last night's row... but Granny will never know, because Lauren will never tell her.

Anyway, Amelia is wrong. She is so wrong. Patrick is the one. Lauren is more certain of that than ever. She needs someone who acts normal, looks normal, has a decent job; someone she can introduce to friends and colleagues. What she doesn't need is someone who disturbs memories, disrupts her life, challenges her career; someone who tries to dig deep inside her... Besides, Clifford Adderman was a heartbreaker, according to Twitter, anyway. Why should Nash Adderman be any different?

'I hope Nash gets his plaster off alright,' says Granny.

'Gold digger,' mutters Patrick.

'At least he didn't ask me what my house was worth,' says Granny.

'I didn't ask you how much it was worth, just if you had had it valued.'

'Sounds like the same thing to me.'

'What I meant,' says Patrick, 'what I meant by "gold digger" is the fact that Nash stayed at *Fois* for six weeks without paying.'

'He can't pay if he doesn't have the money,' Granny replies.

'I bet he does,' says Patrick.

'Do you think so?' Lauren can't help asking from the back.

'People like Nash always have money,' says Patrick. 'Just never on them.'

Lauren pulls his note out of her pocket. IOU 3K. Patrick will be impressed that she's kept evidence of the promise.

'Unsigned,' says Patrick from the front. 'Means nothing, I'm afraid. You may as well throw it away.'

Despite its apparent worthlessness, Lauren shoves the note back into her pocket, but not deep enough, because when they get out at Carlisle services, a gust of wind pulls it out and it flies away. It flaps across the car park and sticks to the windscreen of a parked car.

'Causing chaos even in his absence,' remarks Patrick as they walk past it into the service station.

Lauren takes Patrick's hand and leads him inside, away from the offending note. Then, while he is buying the coffees, Lauren slips back out to the car park and peels the scrap of paper off the windscreen. *It's a hazard*, she tells herself. What's left of it is soft and soggy, and the ink has run so much that it is no longer legible. Lauren screws it up into a ball and walks over to the bin, but once she's there, she can't get her fist to open.

'Lauren!' Patrick has re-emerged from the service station carrying two plastic cups. She chucks the crumpled paper into her bag and follows him back to the car.

* * *

Patrick had envisioned a triumphant return to London. And on the surface, he has got it. Lauren and her grandmother are both in his Jaguar. He has saved them from someone really devious. And yet. As he pulls away from Carlisle services, Patrick feels as if there is someone else intruding on their journey. As if the man that he drove north to displace has slipped into the boot and is poisoning the trip south again.

Even Nash's optimistic and no doubt unrealistic promise of payment felt more like a ransom note. When Patrick watched it flutter across the carpark, it seemed rather sinister, like a malevolent bat.

Added to which, Amelia is becoming the front-seat driver from hell. She was quiet until they reached Carlisle. Now they are on the M6, she is pointing and swearing and shaking her fist at anything that overtakes them.

'How dare you!' she cries, as a juggernaut flies past in the fast lane.

Amelia, Patrick decides, is bonkers. And yet Lauren, as far as he knows, is not. Of course, there is a missing link, between the sane girlfriend and the insane grandmother, and that is the mother. Lauren never talks about her. Was the mother sane or insane?

Women become their mothers. Patrick has read this somewhere. Which means that, had she lived, Lauren's mother would have become like Amelia. So perhaps Lauren is on some sort of trajectory, a well-worn path following in her grandmother's footsteps. Patrick shudders.

'Why do you wear those?' Amelia points at his leather gloves.

'They're for driving.'

'But why?'

'Because... well, because they're comfortable.'

'They look a bit silly.'

Patrick feels irritation rising to the surface. 'Amelia, you are getting a lift home. I advise you not to annoy the driver.'

'You rotters!' Amelia has forgotten her chauffeur and is shaking her fist at the oncoming traffic.

Patrick turns on Radio 3.

* * *

The hospital is quiet. Almost no one in the waiting room. Nash feels relieved. He should get his plaster off in no time. His appointment is at 11.15 and on the dot a nurse appears.

'Mr Adderman?'

Nash gets up and follows the nurse through to the consulting room.

'Good morning,' says the elderly male consultant.

'Good morning,' replies Nash. 'Thank you for this. I tell you, I can't wait to have it off. Or rather get it off. The plaster, I mean.'

'Well then, if you would like to get up on the couch and extend your leg.'

Nash climbs onto the medical couch and stretches his leg out. This is it, the moment he's been waiting for. Six weeks of imprisonment, but now it's over.

'If you could fetch me the saw,' says the consultant to the nurse.

'Saw?' Nash gulps. He can't have heard that correctly.

The nurse leaves the room, returns with what looks like an electric pizza cutter and hands it to the consultant.

'There must be some mistake,' says Nash.

'Are you not Mr Adderman?'

'Yes, but...'

'And is this not your leg?'

'Yes, but,' Nash is sweating profusely, 'That looks like – well, a saw.'

'Saw and vacuum,' corrects the consultant. 'The vacuum hoovers up the mess as we go.'

'No, thank you,' says Nash. 'I think I'll leave it on for now. The plaster, I mean. I've become quite attached to it...'

'Lie still.'

But Nash is up and off the couch and running for the door as fast as a man with a plaster cast can go. The nurse catches up with him in the corridor.

'Come along,' she says. 'I've seen two-year-olds with more courage.'

Nash reluctantly returns to the consulting room where, once the consultant has commandeered two extra nurses to hold the patient still, it only takes a couple of minutes to take the plaster off.

Nash is shocked by his right leg. The plaster has provided a second artificial leg for six whole weeks, so Nash had almost forgotten what was underneath it. And what is revealed is pathetic. A thin, fragile-looking matchstick of a leg. No muscles to speak of, and no hairs either. It looks like a plant that has been grown in the dark – pale and scrawny.

'Is it mine?' he asks.

The nurses laugh but the consultant looks stern and talks about the importance of physiotherapy. Then he gives Nash a letter to take back to his GP. Nash doesn't have a GP; he doesn't believe in them. He only uses alternative medicine. But he decides not to mention this, it would sound a bit ungrateful. Instead he listens to the consultant telling him that it will take time for the muscles in his right leg to recover and how the other leg, the left one, may remain dominant, even though he is right handed.

'So, let's see you walk, Mr Adderman.'

'Sorry?'

'Walk, please! Up and down.'

Nash steps forward with his left leg and drags the right after it, keeping it nice and stiff, so as not to damage the bone in any way.

'I said walk. Walk normally. Bend your knee.'

'It won't bend,' says Nash. And the truth is, he has no idea how to make it. His right leg is straight as a drainpipe, always will be. Anyone can see that.

'Bend your knee!' repeats the consultant.

'I can't.' Nash is sure that walking is possible for other people but... and then suddenly, his right knee bends, stiffly, rustily, like the tin man.

'Put your weight on it!' cries the consultant. 'Forward, march!'

A creak and a groan, and Nash is off, up and down the carpet like a regular robot.

'Success!' says Nash.

'Sort of,' says the consultant. 'It may take a while to get back to normal.'

Nash stares at his leg, willing it back to full functionality. It looks raw and exposed, and Nash can feel its pain.

CHAPTER 10

The day after they get back to London, Lauren wakes in a nervous mood. Something she can't put her finger on. A feeling that she is sure is linked to nostalgia. She often experiences this when she gets back from Loch Fleet, but this time it's worse than usual. The day stretches ahead of her, as empty as a beach when the tide is out, and she is not sure how to fill it.

Patrick goes to the bakery to buy some croissants. Lauren walks round and round the flat, picking things up and putting them down again. Patrick has lovely things. Trinkets, he calls them, inherited from his mother. Silver-framed photographs of women in ball gowns; tiny glass bottles from Venice, red and blue; cut-glass paperweights; porcelain jugs. Finally, Lauren sits down at the kitchen table and gazes out of the window.

Patrick's kitchen is in the basement, and when Lauren looks out, she can only see the street out of the top pane, which means she can only see the bottom half of passers-by. An array of different legs, strolling past.

On summer evenings, Lauren and Patrick look out on the legs while they are eating supper and play a game of guessing who they belong to. Who owns the legs in tartan trousers – a poet or a stockbroker? Does the long skirt and trainers belong to a pop star or a student? They'll never know, but it's fun to guess.

As Lauren sits in the kitchen, waiting for Patrick, she imagines seeing Nash walking past. He would be easy to spot in his shorts and flip-flops. And she wonders how it would feel to see him again.

'Penny for your thoughts?' Patrick has come in silently behind her and put his hands on either side of her shoulders.

'Oh!' Lauren jumps and turns round. 'Oh, it's you. I… just for a moment, I wondered who it was.'

'Good surprise, then?' Patrick laughs. 'I mean that it's me.'

'Gosh, yes! Good surprise!' Lauren says. 'I mean, not a surprise anyway, because this is your flat!' She laughs. 'It's good,' she says. 'Very good.'

A strange silence comes over the kitchen and neither of them can seem to break it.

'Fancy a walk on Hampstead Heath after breakfast?' Patrick says eventually. 'We could go out for lunch afterwards.'

'Oh, yes!' Lauren is full of relief, although she has no idea why. Sunday is planned; their time together organised, and in a good way. A walk on the heath, followed by lunch, probably followed by a quiet evening at home and no doubt a film on the telly.

Patrick puts on the coffee machine and soon the kitchen is full of its aroma. Lovely, Lauren thinks, being back here in London. Everything is great. Calm and organised. She pushes all thoughts of flip flops out of her mind.

* * *

Primrose Hill is a beautiful place to live. Every time she and Patrick walk out of his flat and into Chalcot Square, Lauren is amazed by the pastel-coloured Regency town houses that line the street. Some are painted pale pink, others light blue, yellow or green, as if a gigantic cake-decorator has covered them all with colourful icing.

110

They walk down Regent's Park Road, past cafés thronged with people, over the railway bridge where there used to be a station, and up the hill towards Hampstead Heath.

The heath is busier than usual. Scores of people trekking along the paths, throwing sticks for excitable dogs. Lauren can't help comparing the straggly grass, overcooked from the summer's heat, with the lush green fields around Loch Fleet. But as they get further onto the heath she starts to relax. She had gone to Scotland for the space, but there is space here too. Miles of heathland, sloping away into the distance, topped with trees.

They pass Hampstead Ponds, fringed with long grasses. The water is calm and still, just the occasional crease on its surface made by a water beetle or dragonfly. On the path ahead of them, a man and a woman are strolling along together with a chihuahua on a lead. They are clearly in love, their arms wrapped tightly around each other.

Lauren takes Patrick's hand. 'It's great to be back,' she begins, uncertainly. 'Isn't it?'

But Patrick is looking further along the path. In the distance a woman is walking towards them. A tall, pale woman with blonde hair and a bold, geometrically patterned shirt.

'Is that Veronica?' Lauren asks.

'Um,' Patrick replies. 'I believe it is.'

As Veronica approaches, Lauren notices a slight tic starting in Patrick's left cheek. At the same time, Patrick begins to release his grip on her hand – slowly, slowly – so that by the time she reaches them, his hand is swinging loosely at his side.

'Hey guys!' Veronica smiles at them both, but she only looks at Patrick.

'Hey!' Patrick has a broad grin on, the one he uses for his clients.

'So how was Scotland?'

'Great!' Lauren and Patrick say it together and too quickly, as if it's been rehearsed, even though it hasn't.

'What was great?' asks Veronica, as if she senses something amiss.

'It's a lovely place,' says Patrick.

'Good.'

'Although...' Patrick begins, then stops.

'The weather wasn't marvellous,' Lauren says, before Patrick can say anything else.

'Right,' says Veronica. 'Well, I'll see you tomorrow, Patrick.' She nods at Lauren and walks on.

Lauren and Patrick continue their stroll. But it feels to Lauren as if Veronica has taken the fun out of it. She realises she doesn't want to carry on in the direction that Veronica has come from. 'Actually, I feel quite hungry now,' Lauren says.

'What, already? After two croissants?' Patrick laughs.

'Could we try that new restaurant, the one in Belsize Park?'

'Sure.'

In fact the restaurant is more of a deli, but it has a nice vibe about it. There is wood everywhere and a big counter near the door, crammed full of delicacies like venison pie and duck pâté. Lauren likes the stripped pine benches, the wheel back chairs and the wooden panelling, but for some reason the venison and the duck pâté turn her stomach. She averts her eyes and concentrates on the tables at the back. Most are taken by customers, but there is one free next to the Ladies.

'Go and grab it,' says Patrick. 'I'll find some menus.'

Lauren plonks her coat on one chair and her bag on another, then she goes into the toilet. In the mirror her face looks tired and white. Not the sort of face that's just spent a week at the coast. She gives her cheeks a little pinch and returns to the table where Patrick is sitting reading the menu.

'There's chicken chasseur, salade niçoise, or a thing with beans,' he says, looking up at her. 'Not a great choice, but anyway.' He folds the menu away. 'Shall we go for the chicken?'

'I'll have the thing with beans,' says Lauren.

'But why? I thought you liked chicken chasseur?'

'I do, but… well, I feel like a change.'

'You always say it's a waste not having a meat dish when we're out.'

'I'll have the chicken next time.'

Patrick picks up the menu again and opens it irritably. 'Five types of beans,' he reads. He peers closer at the text. 'It's a stew,' he adds. 'A cold one.'

'I don't feel like meat,' Lauren explains.

Patrick purses his lips together. 'Is it because of that vegan?' he asks, not taking his eyes off the menu.

'What vegan?'

'The Nash vegan.'

'Of course not,' replies Lauren defensively.

'Because…' But Patrick doesn't finish his sentence. Instead he waves the waiter over and orders chicken chasseur for himself, and the thing with beans for Lauren.

* * *

There's usually a moment when things go wrong. When a relationship teeters like a wavering line of dominoes. The days, weeks and months are lined up along the carpet, testament to hard work and staying power, built up slowly, domino by domino. But if one should fall, it knocks into the one before and the one before that, until the carpet is just one long collapsed wall of dominoes.

Lauren is just right, Patrick tells himself. *Perfect for me in every way.* Now they are back in London, he and Lauren are getting on just fine. No better or worse than usual. There hasn't been a bad omen, a feeling of dread, or an

113

awkwardness in the bedroom. Yet as he watches Lauren negotiating her five-bean stew, Patrick's mind follows Veronica striding over the heath with her bobbed hair and her colourful shirt, and he wonders if the moment has arrived.

* * *

Nourishing Noodles

This recipe is going to be difficult. It's going to focus on your vulnerable side. After all, we've all got one. Yes – even you.

I was introduced to mine just a few days ago. When my plaster was finally taken off, my leg looked like a noodle. Thin, white, almost transparent in places.

What I didn't realise is that I'd been carting this noodly leg around for weeks, protected by a plaster, and probably disguised by it too.

I'm sure this is true for most of us. I mean, our protection is also our disguise. But what are we hiding? I fear it is our real selves.

Nash pauses, gets up from his desk, rolls up his jeans and makes himself look at his right leg. The hairs are starting to grow back, but the limb is still weedy and pale. He sits back down in front of his typewriter.

Uncooked noodles are hard, inflexible, brittle laces, with an inedible look about them. Cooked with care, they become soft and sensual. Most noodles are vegan, egg noodles being the obvious exception (always check the label). And as an accompaniment, I recommend something hot and spicy.

Ingredients
1-2 onions

2-3 garlic cloves

1 packet of firm tofu

Oodles of soy sauce

A splash of Tabasco

1-2 tbsps grated ginger

1 medium tomato, chopped

1 tin of coconut milk

1 tsp soft brown sugar

Vegetables – whatever you happen to have on the day.
The secret is to chop them small, so they don't take
much time to cook.

Notice I haven't mentioned beansprouts. They are of
course delicious, but unless you buy them fresh, they
tend to ferment in their plastic bags – anyway, no one
wants plastic these days. So leave out the beansprouts,
unless you have time to sprout your own. (See the
appendix for sprouting seeds of all varieties.)

This recipe requires patience and planning. Because I
want you to marinade the tofu in soy sauce and
Tabasco, then leave it in the fridge overnight. This will
give the tofu time to soak up the marinade and
transform it from a bland block of protein that's
squeaky on the teeth into a parcel of delights.

Once your tofu is marinated, you are going to sear it. To
do this, you need to heat some sesame oil in a frying
pan or wok. Add the block of tofu to the hot oil and sear
on both sides. Remove from the wok, cut into decent
chunks and cover to keep warm, ready to add to the stir
fry at the end.

Time to start on the vegetables. Sauté the onions first,
then the garlic, then the grated ginger. You could add a
little soft brown sugar here. Once everything has
softened, begin to add the other vegetables, stirring

them around the wok. Add a few dashes of soy sauce and cover, allowing everything to simmer. If the vegetables start to dry up, add the chopped tomato for moisture, or some coconut milk.

Now for the noodles –

Nash stops again. He is avoiding it, he realises. Like all men, even New Age ones. He is avoiding the notion of vulnerability. He has brought it up, but he's not prepared to continue. Instead he has launched into another recipe.

But what is it, this message that is lurking beneath the surface? It hurts to love, is that it? Sounds more like a warning. But maybe there are similarities between loving and the cooking process. It's hard to go through, if you're a noodle. Trial by boiling, then being sautéed within an inch of your life or even burnt to a crisp, depending on the recipe.

It hurts to change, he types, *ask any noodle.* And then he pauses. No, it's gone. The moment has passed. Inspiration has flown, if indeed it ever landed. He will have to finish for today. Go for a walk, maybe. Find a park to kick leaves around in. Buy himself a vegan latte and steal some ideas for his *Cha, Cha, Chai* section. Crikey, this writing business is hard work. Harder than he thought it would be. Pulling a book out of him like an enormously long noodle. He knows that without his promise, he wouldn't have got this far. And for that he silently thanks her.

* * *

August becomes September, and the sun begins to mellow. Its warm beams shine into Lauren's eyes as she walks from the train station to her grandmother's house. Willowherb seeds fill the air, flying along the street like tiny fairies.

Late summer is lovely in Granny's garden. Lauren helps Amelia pick blackcurrants and make jars of shiny, black jam. In October, they turn fallen apples into chutney; they bottle plums. Or at least Granny does. Lauren watches mostly, sitting at the kitchen table and nursing a mug of tea.

'You're a legend, Granny!'

'You'd be surprised how many others do it.'

For one terrible moment, Lauren thinks that Granny is going to mention Nash. She hasn't so far. His name has been left unspoken, hanging silently in the air. Lauren's hand wobbles and the tea spills onto the table.

But then Granny says: 'Home-grown is all the rage, you know.'

'I know,' Lauren smiles. 'You're right.'

'Of course, Patrick won't have time for growing vegetables,' adds Granny.

'No,' Lauren keeps her smile on, wondering where this is going.

'A wasted opportunity,' Granny says vaguely.

Lauren doesn't ask her to clarify. Since they got back from Scotland, Patrick hasn't offered to come to Croydon and Lauren hasn't suggested it. It seems a good idea to keep him and Granny apart.

In November, Lauren and Granny light a bonfire and stand beside it, sucking treacle toffee, gloved hands in pockets. Granny produces two sparklers and gives one to Lauren. Granny's sparkler ignites into a beautiful line of stars. She waves it in the air, writing the same word over and over. It's a four letter word, but Lauren doesn't look too closely. Her own sparkler doesn't light.

The whole keeping Granny and Patrick apart thing is problematic at Christmas, but Lauren comes up with a solution. She and Patrick will celebrate together on Christmas Eve, and then he will go to his father's and Lauren to her grandmother's on the day. Patrick agrees; they muddle through. They are invited for New Year at Veronica's.

January is cold and wet. Patrick and Lauren survive the dark nights by watching Netflix and ordering takeaways.

February is clear and cold. Twice, Primrose Hill is covered with a dusting of snow, like icing sprinkled on a cake.

Then, at the beginning of March, Lauren misses an apostrophe. An apostrophe on a book cover: the fifth book in Jerbil Publishing's cosy crime series. It's supposed to be called *Eagles' Eyrie*. Except when the hardbacks arrive from the printer, the cover says *Eagles Eyrie*.

Lauren thinks it's because in an earlier editorial meeting, no one could decide where the apostrophe should actually go. Lauren had pointed out that the correct place was after the s, but the designer said that looked unattractive and the apostrophe should go before the s, so it read *Eagle's Eyrie*. Someone else said it was a pity to have any apostrophe at all on a book cover. And then Lauren got distracted and started thinking about the heron on Loch Fleet and how it always got furious when it saw her coming and flew away with a grumpy croak. Lauren pictured the heron flapping slowly over the loch, and suddenly the meeting was over and she hadn't heard what had been decided, so when the proofs arrived and the cover said *Eagles Eyrie*, Lauren went with it without checking.

When they unpack the books the night before the launch, everyone is distraught. The writer is tearful, the editor furious and the accountant glum. No one blames Lauren directly, but it's clearly her fault. Lauren doesn't sleep for a week. She lies tossing and turning, wishing she could put the apostrophe back.

Lauren is worried that one mistake could lead to another, that she is losing her grip. And she worries that Nash was right. That there is the slimmest, slightest chance that she is in the wrong job.

The following Friday, a week to the day since the fatal cockup, Lauren confides in Camilla.

'I can't seem to concentrate. It's like the words jump about now. Sometimes the letters, too.'

'Are you getting enough sleep?'

'Are you joking? I get no sleep at all.'

'Well don't start taking pills,' warns Camilla. 'Try something alternative.'

An image of Nash healing her houseplants leaps into Lauren's mind. 'I'm not trying reiki.'

'Ok, not reiki. Reflexology maybe?' suggests Camilla.

'I don't know anyone who does it.'

'There's someone around the corner from here. A Mr Bryant.'

'How do you know?'

'I pass his house every morning,' Camilla replies. 'He's got a sign on the gate.'

'I'm not that desperate,' Lauren replies. And the conversation moves on.

But she must be. Because later that afternoon, Lauren phones Mr Bryant and he says he can help her insomnia. But he doesn't promise to fix it; he promises to address it. He explains that bodies heal themselves, and that reflexology will remind her body how to do it. It doesn't sound very hopeful, but Lauren has no other options. She agrees to try.

* * *

That evening there is yet another dinner at Veronica's. Although it passes quickly, thank goodness. Lauren has only just managed to swallow her teeny, tiny steak. Funny how she finds meat hard to chew these days. She used to love steak before... well, never mind.

All around her, the noise of conversation is growing. Happy North London professionals, replete with food and wine, have pulled off their napkins, pushed back their chairs and started to relax. Someone has even got out an e-cigarette.

'How's work going?' Veronica has appeared from nowhere and is smiling at Lauren.

'Oh, fine, fine,' Lauren mumbles. Lauren is certain that Veronica has a trouble-seeking radar. Veronica never normally asks her about her job. Now Lauren has problems at work, Veronica seems to sense it.

'It just takes one slip as a proofreader, doesn't it?' says Veronica, as she hands Lauren a cheese plate.

'I don't want any cheese.'

'Some grapes then,' says Veronica, forcing the plate into Lauren's hand. *This is my house*, Veronica is implying. *I'm the boss here.*

Lauren accepts the plate and then ignores it, turning to her right where two people she doesn't know are discussing some sort of deal.

'Quite a bidding war,' says a woman with long, red hair. 'But we were successful in the end.'

'How much?' asks the man opposite with thick-rimmed glasses.

'That would be telling,' smiles the woman. 'Let's hope it sells.'

'Why wouldn't it? Veganism is taking off.'

Lauren's ears prick up. 'Do you work in catering?' she asks the woman.

'Catering!' The red-haired woman looks horrified. 'No, publishing. We're talking about a cookery book.'

'A vegan one,' says the spectacled man. 'Sarah here has just signed an author for what she hopes will be a best-selling book.'

'Out next year,' smiles Sarah.

Lauren thinks about Nash, hunched over his typewriter, bashing out his mad ideas for an obscure publisher in Nebraska. What was his publisher called again? Before the Bear. Nash will never be a best-selling author; anyone can see that. And every time a new cookery book comes out, especially a vegan one, it will push Nash further from his goal. And Lauren feels gutted. Not for him, no – of course not for him. *It's not that I care about Nash. It's just because he owes me money*, she tells herself.

The conversation next to her moves on to celebrity memoirs but Lauren has had enough. She's tired and she wants to go home. She looks around the table for Patrick and realises he's not there. Lauren gets up and wanders into the kitchen. Patrick is bending over the open dishwasher, loading dinner plates. Veronica is leaning against the worktop, chatting.

'And then you'll never guess what happened,' Veronica is saying.

'Can we go?' Lauren interrupts.

Patrick looks up from his task. 'Sure.' But he carries on loading the plates, like an obedient husband.

'Now,' says Lauren. 'I'm tired, Patrick.'

'Right.' Patrick straightens up and shuts the dishwasher. 'I'll go and find our coats.'

'Is everything alright?' Veronica asks.

'Of course,' Lauren replies.

* * *

When the reflexologist opens the door, Lauren is expecting a shiny salon with polished floors and mirrors. Instead she steps into a dimly lit hall with a wooden floor and patterned wallpaper.

'Come this way.' Mr Bryant leads Lauren down the hall and into a room on the right. In the middle of the room, a padded garden chair sits straight-backed and covered with the sort of paper therapists use. On the wall beside the door an enormous bookcase groans with books. *Stonehenge Up Close* reads one cover. *Inside the Human Body* says another. A strange unease creeps up Lauren's neck and makes her scalp tingle.

Mr Bryant gestures to the chair. 'If you would like to remove your socks and shoes and then take a seat,' he says.

Lauren bends down to untie her bootlaces. When she takes off her boots and socks, her feet look strange, as if they don't belong to her, the skin creased from the wool pattern of the socks. Lauren sits on the chair and the paper sheets detach themselves underneath her. She wishes she hadn't come.

'Sit back a bit,' Mr Bryant says. He waits for Lauren to push herself further into the chair, then he tips it slowly and carefully backwards until her head is facing the ceiling.

'So, we've done the paperwork.' The reflexologist walks round to the front of the chair and plonks himself on a low stool at her feet.

Lauren swallows nervously. 'Paperwork?'

'The online form I sent you.'

'Oh yes.'

'And you're still not sleeping?'

'Not at all.'

Mr Bryant takes hold of Lauren's left foot. Despite her unease, there is something about the way he does it that is instantly reassuring. *I've got you*, the grasp says. She silently hands herself over.

The reflexologist starts working, holding Lauren's left foot in his left hand and running his right thumb up and down it in a way that makes her toes tingle.

'You can relax,' he says. Lauren opens her eyes and looks at him. 'Keep your eyes closed, and try to relax.'

Lauren shuts her eyelids again with a snap.

'You're carrying too much,' Mr Bryant says. 'Too much stuff. Can you feel it on your shoulders?'

'Maybe.'

'You need to let it slide off. Like taking off a rucksack.'

Lauren tries to imagine it, but draws a blank.

'It's a canvas bag,' the reflexologist says. 'With leather straps. The straps are loose and they are sliding slowly down your arm. Loosening the load.'

There is a sudden clunk on the wooden floor. Lauren's eyes spring open.

'Eyes closed,' he says again.

Lauren's shoulders are suddenly free. Her arms feel light and fluffy, as if they are made of air. They start to float up from her sides.

'Better?'

Lauren nods but keeps her eyes closed. Lights are zooming at the back of her eyelids, lovely balls of pink and yellow, and she doesn't want to lose them.

Mr Bryant moves down to the fleshy part of the sole. This feels more uncomfortable. Lauren can feel his thumb, strong and constant, moving with a strange wiggle like a caterpillar. Then something feels crunchy, as if there are granules under the skin. She opens one eye.

'Toxins,' the therapist says. 'We can break them down.'

His thumb works harder, the pressure increases. A sudden stab of pain, and her foot feels smooth again.

Lauren's breathing is slowing; she feels her chest rising up and down. *Windbag.* The word pops into her mind, then splits into two. *Wind. Bag. Wind. Bag...*

'That's you all done.'

Lauren wakes with a jolt from a beautiful dream. She was on the shore of Loch Fleet, the sea lapping against it, gorse bushes swaying in the breeze.

'So, um, how was everything?' she asks.

'I think the problem is coming from your heart.'

Lauren sits up quickly, the chair folds upright and the torn protective paper flops onto the floor.

The reflexologist smiles gently. 'Not your actual heart. Your heart energy.' He picks the protective paper off the floor, crumples it into a ball and looks at the clock. 'There is something hiding in your heart,' he says simply. 'And this is where the insomnia is coming from.'

'What can you do about it?' Lauren asks.

Mr Bryant smiles again and shakes his head. 'Well... the reflexology will help, of course, but–' he hesitates, '–it's *your* heart.'

* * *

When Lauren gets home from the reflexologist, she does something she told herself she would never do. She opens her laptop and types *Clifford Adderman* into Twitter.

It comes up straight away – the post by Hannah Strawlight. *I can never forgive Clifford Adderman.* But instead of the confession she was expecting, Lauren finds a link to a newspaper article. Crikey, whatever Nash did to Hannah Strawlight, it made the paper. Thrilled and horrified in equal measure, Lauren clicks on the link and is immediately confronted with a photo of a much younger Nash, standing in what looks like the kitchen of a busy restaurant, wearing a chef's whites and hat. Underneath the photo is Hannah's article.

I can never forgive Clifford Adderman. For he has broken my heart. Twice. Firstly, by leaving the best restaurant in London. Secondly, by becoming vegan. Yes – vegan! And as I am the most bloodthirsty food critic in the capital, I will never taste his cooking again.

The next paragraph explains to the reader what a fantastic cook Clifford *was* when he cooked properly. There are photos, too. Simmering stews, succulent roasts and what looks like a pistachio quiche.

After describing some of his mouth-watering dishes, Hannah goes on to claim that Clifford Adderman has not just ruined her life; he has ruined his own as well. Or his career, anyway. *No one eats vegan*, Hannah explains to the reader. *It's disgusting stuff. A fad that will never last.* But Hannah doesn't stop there. She writes that veganism is not just a fad, it's a cult. One that has ensnared Clifford, and brainwashed him, too. She makes a few jokey suggestions that might save Clifford from his terrible fate. She even invites her foody friends to invade Vegan HQ and kidnap him before it's too late. Then she finishes with a dire warning. *Unless he sees the error of his ways, Clifford Adderman will never work again. Not in London anyway.*

Lauren looks at the date at the top of the article. 2005. Eleven years ago. An image pops into her mind. Nash standing on the beach, his mouth twisted into a strange sort of smile. 'I'm too *avant garde* for my own good.'

Lauren shuts her laptop. If only Nash *had* broken Hannah Strawlight's heart. If only he *was* a cad and a bounder. It would make everything so much easier. But she doesn't let herself consider what *everything* is. Lauren walks round and round the apartment, picking up objects and putting them down again, wishing Patrick was home, trying not to think.

* * *

Patrick sighs with frustration. Why is the North Circular such a nightmare? There is always a problem with the traffic. If not a lane closure then a breakdown – something to cause delays and tailbacks. Today, in their wisdom, workmen have removed the white lines dividing the three lanes, slowing cars down to a crawl. Patrick sighs again.

It's not good, this delay. It gives him too much time for thinking. Patrick pushes Lauren out of his mind before abruptly switching to what looks like a smaller queue. It's a smart move, and Patrick is soon speeding towards his destination.

'You're late!'

'Don't be cross, Veronica. It's taken me hours to get here.'

'Yes, but I have the beautician coming soon to paint my nails.'

'Any particular colour?'

'You are sweet – I mean, feigning an interest! You're very good at it.'

'Good at what?' Patrick pulls Veronica towards him, searching for her mouth.

'Not so fast. I want to unpack my last dinner party with you.'

'Oh.' Patrick stops trying to kiss Veronica and rubs his eyes. 'Well, it was great.'

'What was great?'

'The food. Everything. It was all great.'

'Lauren was quiet.'

'Was she? I don't remember. I don't think she's sleeping well.'

'She hasn't guessed, has she?'

'Look, Veronica, I can't do this if... if you keep mentioning Lauren.'

'I'm sorry. It's just...'

'Can we go up?'

'Of course.' Veronica takes Patrick's hand and leads him upstairs.

* * *

Lauren gives up waiting for Patrick. She skips supper and crawls into bed. She lies with her eyes closed, willing sleep to come. Then suddenly she's gone. Back to *Fois*. Nash is there, she can hear him typing in his room, but she can't get his door to open and he doesn't hear her knocking. Lauren leaves him in peace and wanders down to the beach.

A flock of oystercatchers is standing on the sandy shore. Lauren inches towards them, closer and closer, and then – oh joy – she's among them, and she looks down to see she has webbed feet and feathers and—

'Lauren!' Patrick's voice. 'You've overslept.'

'What time is it?'

'Ten to nine.'

'Why didn't you wake me?'

'I'm sorry. I wasn't sure...'

Lauren leaps out of bed and starts frantically trying to dress. It's Friday. The morning of Jerbil Publishing's weekly editorial meeting. The one day of the week when everyone arrives at work at nine o'clock instead of half past. And she is going to be late.

Five minutes later, she's running to Chalk Farm underground station. The lift is jammed so she takes the stairs. Down, down she runs. By the time she reaches the bottom and dashes to the platform, it's ten past nine. She looks up at the sign. *Next Edgware train 8 minutes*. And then it's cancelled. *Next Edgware train 15 minutes* blinks the sign. It feels like another dream, this time a bad one.

Finally, at ten past ten, Lauren stumbles into the office. The meeting has just finished. The other women in the team are switching off their laptops and packing their bags. Camilla is stacking the dirty cups and saucers. She gives Lauren a look of warning.

'Well!' says Caroline, the Editorial Director. 'I have to say that we missed you this morning.'

'I'm so sorry. I overslept.'

'I mean we missed your presentation.'

'Sorry?'

'It was your turn.'

'Was it?' Lauren realises she has no recollection of whatever it was she was supposed to prepare.

'Why don't we have a chat,' Caroline says.

Lauren follows her back into the meeting room.

'It seems to me you've lost your spark,' says Caroline, once she's closed the door. 'You used to be, well... much more conscientious.'

'I haven't been sleeping...' Lauren begins.

'Until today!'

'Well, yes, until today.'

'Forgive me, Lauren, but it feels as if you're losing interest in your job.'

Lauren opens her mouth to deny it, then shuts it again.

'Perhaps it's not enough for you anymore?'

'But I love publishing!'

'Publishing, perhaps. But proofreading? I'm not sure it's satisfying you like it used to.'

Lauren stays silent.

'I mean, there was your mistake over the apostrophe – a costly one as it turned out – and there have been other ones, too. Smaller mistakes, so I let them go thinking it was a phase you were going through, but they haven't stopped—'

'What mistakes?'

Caroline waves her hand dismissively. 'Just things that a proofreader should notice. Things that you used to notice. So, what I want to know is – what's going on?'

Lauren's head is crowded with thoughts, whirring round and round like leaves flying from a tree, and then: 'I see myself working with people,' she replies. 'Rather than words.' And as she says it, Lauren promises herself that if she ever sees Nash again, she will kill him.

'Is this a resignation speech?' laughs Caroline. But Lauren can hear relief in her laugh. And she feels it too. As if something heavy has fallen off her back. A rucksack perhaps.

* * *

After her chat with Caroline the day passes in a blur. Lauren has a much longer meeting with Human Resources, and together they plan her future with Jerbil Publishing. It is agreed that Lauren will finish her current projects or work one month's notice, whichever is the shorter. She will stay on the company books as a freelancer, with first refusal on new proofreading projects. And she will be notified of editorial openings. No preferential treatment, but a heads-up in advance of any advertisements in the trade papers. As they talk, Lauren keeps seeing Nash's Get Out of Jail Free card in her head.

Finally it's over, and Lauren is walking up the road from Chalk Farm station. She has come home early. Everyone agreed that there was no point in her staying till five. Not today. She'll have a good rest over the weekend and go back on Monday. Make a fresh start. Lauren feels less free now, more empty. She tells herself it's a good thing; it means there's room for something new. She just doesn't know what that is yet.

* * *

Patrick has always been risk-averse. His clients and his colleagues appreciate his prudence. No one wants a lawyer who is impulsive or daring. Caution is the name of the game, at least for those that constantly want to win it.

But when it comes to sex, Patrick has always enjoyed a bit of risk-taking. Not bondage or anything like that. Just a whiff of danger, a feeling that an intimate moment might be disturbed. *In flagrante delicto*. The first Latin phrase that he learned at school. *Caught in the act.*

It's just a fantasy, of course. Patrick has no intention of getting caught. Which is why when the doorbell goes on his little *tête-à-tête* with Veronica, he doesn't get out of bed to answer it.

'Could be a delivery,' says Veronica.

'They'll come back.'

Patrick silently thanks Amazon, Ocado, whoever it is. He was flagging slightly, and the sudden fear of discovery has rekindled his desire.

But then there is the sound of a key turning in the lock, the creak of the front door opening and the unmistakable sound of Lauren dropping her bag in the hall.

Patrick looks at Veronica. She looks back. As one, the two lovers slip silently out of bed. Patrick bends to pick up his boxers; Veronica creeps towards the en suite.

A sound of footsteps in the corridor. 'Patrick?'

He experiences a sort of déjà vu. A life review of his relationship with Lauren. He remembers meeting her on top of Primrose Hill; their first date; the fishing holiday when he fell in the river; their trip to Tuscany. The way she laughs, her terrible cooking, the fact that no one before her had...

And then the door opens.

* * *

Strange how Lauren initially notices the details. The obvious thing to look at is Veronica, stark naked and reversing towards the bathroom. Yet the thing Lauren clocks first is Veronica's bracelet – a chunky silver bangle, the sort of thing you would find for sale in an expensive hotel. Lauren has always quite liked the bangle, even imagined wearing it, and now here it is in her bedroom. It's lying on Patrick's side of the bed and Lauren realises how glad she is that it's on his bedside table and not hers. She would be livid if it was on her side. They have a thing about not leaving things on each other's side of the bed. Only yesterday morning, Patrick pointedly lifted a nail file off his bedside table and put it on Lauren's. And she wonders what Patrick feels; whether he is just a little bit annoyed that Veronica has put her bangle on his side. Because a bangle is much bigger than a nail file.

It's easier to concentrate on details. It saves Lauren having to think about the big picture. She will have to think about it, of course, in another second or two; and Patrick will have to look at *her*, rather than at Veronica, who is bent over the worst of her nakedness and still reversing towards the open bathroom door. Then Lauren notices another detail. Veronica has grabbed something on her way, and it's trailing along the carpet, and the thing is Lauren's turquoise bathrobe. And that's when Lauren opens her mouth and screams. She can't help it – the bathrobe is the last straw. It's quite new and only recently washed and it's definitely hers, not to be shared with anyone else. And now she's livid after all, so livid that the first thing she says when she's finished screaming is addressed to Veronica rather than Patrick.

'How many times have you worn it?'

Veronica turns red, which is strange because Lauren has only ever seen her pale before, but she doesn't reply.

'Roughly?' Lauren snarls.

'I'm so sorry, Lauren.' Patrick's voice. He has finally managed to look at her, but she can't look back.

Veronica has made it to the en suite. Lauren knows she won't dare to re-emerge wearing the bathrobe and the towels are in the wash, which means that in order to come out she will have to wear the bathmat.

'It won't happen again,' Patrick says.

Lauren glares at him. 'What won't? Are we talking about renting out my bathrobe, or sleeping with Veronica?' Veronica is a great word to say in anger: she practically spits it out.

It won't happen again. Open to interpretation. It could mean *We won't do it here again, only at hers,* or it could mean *Don't worry, I'll buy her a bathrobe.* Patrick knows that she is a proofreader and proofreaders understand just as much about words as lawyers do – more, maybe. And then Lauren remembers that she's not really a proofreader anymore. She realises that on one single day she has managed to lose a job and a boyfriend, not to mention a home.

'Can you bring me my clothes?' says Veronica from the bathroom. She doesn't dare add *Patrick.*

'No!' Lauren shouts.

Patrick sits down on the bed and silently blinks. Lauren realises that the last time she was this angry was with Nash, and suddenly she is sobbing. Because what is squatting in someone's cottage for six weeks compared to being unfaithful to your girlfriend of three years.

'I loved you, Lauren.'

Patrick has used the past tense, and this makes Lauren angry again. 'You didn't, Patrick.'

'I did.'

'No, Patrick, you didn't.' Strange how now she's said it, it feels so true. And suddenly Nash is there in the bedroom beside her.

Perhaps Patrick can sense Nash too, because he asks, 'Who've you got this from?'

His presumption that someone else has had to point it out, that for three whole years she was too stupid to realise, makes Lauren even more furious. 'You will never love anyone!' she cries. 'Not properly, anyway.' It seems only fair to borrow Nash's words. After all, he owes her big time.

Patrick doesn't deny it. He just blinks silently back. 'I didn't know what to do about you,' he finally says.

In the en suite, the toilet flushes.

CHAPTER 11

Lauren moves in with Granny. She has nowhere else to go. And the best thing about Croydon is its distance from Primrose Hill.

She needs time on her own. She wants to isolate, crawl away, hide in a lair and lick her wounds. Granny's house is the perfect retreat. Lauren spends her days in the garden, protected by its high walls from nosy neighbours. She lies on the grass and watches the clouds. She feels wonderfully numb. Like an ice cube. She's hoping she'll never feel again.

And she does a few things. Firstly, she changes her phone. She doesn't want Patrick contacting her with questions like *Are you doing ok?* She doesn't want to hear from him again. Or anyone else for that matter. And she comes off social media. She deletes everything. Facebook, Instagram and, last but by no means least, her Twitter account. She doesn't want to see what *anyone* is doing.

Of course, it's not enough. She has to do that one last thing. Difficult to contemplate now she's giving up her job. But at the moment, it's an open door between… well, between now and then. If she's really to cut herself off from everything, she will have to add this to the list. Even though she can't afford it. Lauren picks up her new mobile and dials Sian's number.

'Hello?' Sian's warm, sing-song voice.

'It's Lauren.'

'Lauren! You've changed your phone. How are you doing?'

'I'm ok, thanks. And you?'

'Och, I'm always good, me. Long time, no hear. *Fois* been quiet, has it?'

'Yes.' A pause. 'Actually, that's why I'm phoning. You see, I've decided not to let it. At least not for a bit.'

'Oh?'

'I know this affects you and I'm sorry, I really am.'

'Is your Granny ill?'

'No.'

'What, then?'

'I just need a break—'

'Well, it's your house, of course. I can't pretend I'm not disappointed though. I've been really grateful for the work.'

'I know, Sian. I realise. That's why I wanted to…'

'I'll have to look elsewhere, you'll understand, so I might not be available next time.'

'I know. I mean, I understand. I feel really bad, Sian.'

'And how will *you* manage, Lauren? It's not a cheap place to maintain with no one in it… Wait a minute – this isn't about that Nash, is it?'

'Of course not.'

'Sounds like it might be. You know he's got a book out?'

'Sorry?'

'That book he wrote, it's going to be published.'

'But only in Nebraska,' says Lauren.

'No, in the UK.'

'Really? How do you know?'

'He messaged me,' says Sian. 'Apparently it's already available on pre-order.'

'What's it called?'

'Vegan something or other.

* * *

As soon as she has finished her phone call, Lauren googles *Vegan Recipes for New Age Men*. A blank book cover looms into view.

The text below the book says that the hardback is available to pre-order for £20. Publication in February 2017. And the name of the author is printed underneath in bold type. NASH ADDERMAN.

Twenty quid! And the bastard hasn't paid his rent! Fury is growing in Lauren like a pan about to boil over. Nash has used her. For his own advancement; his own career. First he 'borrowed' her house to write his book in, then he nicked her recipe idea. He even stole the title she suggested. And it must have been a good title, because Nash now has a UK publisher. A publisher called Few Flies. Lauren has never heard of them, but they look much bigger and better than Before the Bear.

She remembers Veronica's dinner party and the conversation about the bidding war. And she realises that it was Nash's book they must have been talking about – *Nash* has been given an enormous advance for his stupid, stupid book. Well, she will email Few Flies and tell them about Nash's debt. That will give them a shock when they discover that their debut author is a nasty piece of work. But she'd better check her bank balance first, just to be absolutely sure. Lauren opens her laptop and logs onto internet banking.

And there it is, a credit of three thousand pounds, paid in this morning. The reference says NASH. As good as his word, he's paid her Christmas rates.

* * *

Nash only feels better for a second, which is a great pity. He thought he would feel great for ages. As he walked into his bank, he had felt on top of the world. He could pay the debt. Finally. Completely. He even thought about adding more, but something stopped him. He knew Lauren would consider it patronising.

Of course, it wasn't just about the money, it was also a way to make contact. Now Lauren had changed her phone and taken *Fois* off the letting website, he had no other way. Luckily he still had her bank details from when he hired the house, so unless she had changed those too he could at least give her the money. Back. After all, this was not a charitable donation. It was money he owed and that he should have paid months ago. But making the transfer felt like waving at Lauren, even if from a distance.

However, once the money has left his account and the smiling clerk has given him a slip to prove it has gone, Nash starts to worry. Was every digit correct? Would Lauren actually receive the money? Would she notice? There was no way of knowing.

'You definitely put NASH as the reference?' Nash asks the clerk for the third time.

'Of course, Mr Adderman.'

'Please call me Clifford.'

'I put NASH, Clifford.'

'Right.'

Nash imagines the money in the air, hundreds of notes with tiny wings, zooming from his bank to hers. He sees them flying not across London, but across Loch Fleet, buffeted by a southerly breeze. A lovely image, and then it is gone.

* * *

Simmering Stock Pots

Have you ever met someone you can't forget? Do you have feelings for them constantly simmering under the surface? If you do, you are the perfect person to try this simmering stock pot recipe. In fact, you should always have a stock pot on the go! This is the most environmental recipe in the book because it uses up all the vegetable peelings and stalks that, unless you have a garden and a compost, it is hard to know what to do with. And the great thing is you can be simmering your stock pot while you are cooking something else.

Ingredients
Any kind of peelings, stalks, the ends of carrots, asparagus etc. In other words, anything discarded that is part of a vegetable
A couple of sticks of celery, chopped
A few bay leaves
Salt and pepper

Fling all the ingredients into a saucepan, cover with water and simmer until the vegetables are soft. And while it is simmering, indulge yourself. Think of the person who has captured your feelings. Imagine you are cooking the stock for them. It's hard to tell when stock is ready, and it can often take at least an hour or two of simmering. Plenty of time to remember that special someone...

When you think the stock might be done, sieve it into a jug or jar and keep it in the fridge. Use for diluting sauces or making soups.

The French call a stock 'bouillon'. But they're wrong. Because 'bouillir' means to boil, and you must not allow this to happen! DO NOT LET YOUR STOCK BOIL OVER. Let it simmer gently, and as it simmers, send good thoughts and blessings in a certain direction. They are sure to come back to you, sooner or later.

* * *

Now Lauren isn't working, her mornings have a different shape. She gets up and mooches around in her dressing gown, thinking about the day ahead with all its endless possibilities. She has a coffee while she decides what to do. And then another. But if she waits too long, the moment passes – the moment when she can jump in the shower, get dressed and dry her hair. And suddenly the whole getting-up process seems too long, or too complicated. So it doesn't happen. Lauren stays in her dressing gown and the day drifts by. And then it's dark and time for bed and she promises herself that the next day will be different. But it seldom is.

At least she is three thousand pounds better off, and there was never a better time for that to happen. But there is something strange and impersonal about Nash's financial transaction. As if he has left a party without saying goodbye. Still, it's no surprise when she has done everything to stop him getting in touch.

Granny leaves her alone. Or just the right amount of alone. Amelia makes meals, but she doesn't force Lauren into a ritualistic affair, involving questions like *How's your day?* Granny puts the TV on loud and sits in front of it. When Lauren appears she says, 'I made too much,' or 'There's still some in the oven,' without taking her eyes off the telly.

One morning, Lauren doesn't even get out of bed. She lies for ages watching the sun trace patterns on the ceiling.

'Lunch!' Granny calls, up the stairs.

There is no telly on in the kitchen this time, instead Granny is listening to the radio. A cookery programme, by the sound of it. When Lauren appears, Granny opens the oven and brings out a baking tray of oven chips.

'Are we having eggs with them?'

'I forgot.' Granny looks lost for a minute, then she opens the fridge and finds the eggs.

Lauren suspects that Granny is going off eggs. She still uses them, but not as much, and when she breaks them into a bowl or a frying pan, Lauren notices that Amelia looks away, as if she doesn't want to think about what she's doing.

'Don't worry, there aren't any chicks in there,' Lauren had said, only the other day.

'I know,' Granny had replied. 'But there could have been...'

Is it because of that vegan? Lauren can hear Patrick's question in her head.

'Do you want to grab some knives and forks?' says Granny.

'Ok.' Lauren tugs open the ancient kitchen drawer to find the cutlery, and Granny opens the egg box.

'And now for something completely different,' says the radio presenter. 'Please welcome Nash Adderman.'

'Nash!' cries Granny. She closes the egg box and sits down on a chair to listen.

'I'm so delighted to be here!' Lauren can tell that Nash is beaming at the studio audience.

'It's a long time since you've been on a cookery programme,' the presenter says. 'And you have a new name now?'

'Yes, it's Nash, which is Old English for Cliff.'

'What was wrong with Clifford?' asks the presenter.

'Clifford was a carnivore,' Nash replies.

'I see,' replies the presenter. 'Well, I remember Clifford, and I quite liked him if I'm honest. I liked his recipes, anyway. Where did he go? I mean, where did *you* go?'

'I was in the wilderness,' laughs Nash. 'Literally!'

'Ha!' cries Granny. She stands and starts serving up the chips. The eggs are completely forgotten.

'You were in the wilderness?' repeats the presenter. 'But why?'

'I turned vegan,' says Nash. 'I know it's a thing now, but it wasn't then. I stopped cooking meat, fish or dairy. And,' he hesitates, 'the work dried up.' A pause. 'So I disappeared.'

'But now you're back in the public eye. And cooking again, I presume?'

'Yes, but only vegan now. And I've written a book.'

'So I hear. Can you tell us a bit about it?' '

'Of course. How long have you got?' Nash replies.

'Not long,' says the presenter, taking Nash's joke literally. 'About five minutes.'

'Well it's not out till next year,' says Nash. 'But it's a revolutionary idea.'

'Revolutionary?'

'You see, it combines vegan recipes with a New Age lifestyle. A new concept in cookery books.'

'Really?' The presenter seems less sure. 'Well, we've just got time for an extract.'

'Perfect. I'll read a bit from chapter one.' Nash clears his throat. 'Have you ever seen a woman run?' he asks. 'I mean really run. Flying like the wind beside a stormy sea. Wild running, that's what it looks like. You can live like that. And you can cook like that too...'

Lauren can't move. She feels as though someone has stabbed her in the chest.

'Turn it off, Granny,' she says helplessly. 'Please turn it off.'

* * *

They start climbing together, but Esther's shoes keep filling with sand and Lauren is the first to reach the top of the dunes. Up here, the strength of the breeze is startling. Lauren stands, brushing the sand off her swimsuit, watching the waves crash onto the shore. The beach is deserted, no one for miles in either direction.

'Can I go in?' Lauren cries, as soon as her mother appears. They both know it's not really a question.

Esther laughs, head back, letting the wind shake her long hair out behind her. 'Go on, then!'

And Lauren is off, running, running towards the sea.

For a second Esther stands there watching. Then she

jumps down the dune and races after her daughter. 'Wait for me!' As she runs, Esther pulls off her shoes, then her jumper, then her shorts. She follows Lauren into the waves. 'Wait, Lauren! You have to hold my hand.'

When they come out, their teeth are chattering. Esther picks up her discarded clothes. 'Take this.' Esther hands Lauren her own jumper. It's quite sandy, but at least it's dry. Lauren pulls it over her head. The sleeves hang down much longer than her arms, the ends covering her hands.

'Thank you!'

'No, thank you! I wouldn't have gone in if you hadn't. You're amazing, Lauren!'

'No, you're amazing!'

'Let's go home and change.'

They walk the short distance back to Fois, *hugging each other to keep warm. Giggling from the exertion of running and swimming and the chill of the sea.*

* * *

It's almost two hours since the cookery programme but Lauren hasn't stopped crying. 'That could have been me!'

'I think it probably was,' says Granny.

'But that's the point. It wasn't. I mean, it was for ten minutes, maybe twenty. The wild and carefree Lauren. Running into the wind. But what about the rest of the time? What about now, and tomorrow, and the day after?'

'Exactly.'

'What do you mean *exactly*? I can't live like this, Granny. I can't live like… I don't know, like a mouse.'

'A mouse in mourning,' says Granny. 'I held my tongue while you grieved for Mr Driving Gloves…'

'I wasn't mourning *him*. It was everything. My job, my life… I don't know. Things.'

'But not the things you should have been mourning.'

'What do you mean?'

'You never have. Not properly. I should have insisted. Kept you off school longer. It's just... I was mourning, too.'

And now Granny is crying as well. Enormous teardrops. Lauren has never seen her cry before. It's like rain following a drought – fat drops of rain that make everything wet.

'No wonder you've got stuck,' Granny wails. 'You should have had counselling. You could have had counselling. There was so much other stuff going on, we never got round to it.'

'I still could.'

'What?'

'Get counselling. Although it feels too late.'

'Better late than never. And you've got the money now.'

Lauren is silent and then: 'I'm scared, Granny. You know, lifting the lid...'

'I know.' Amelia is silent for a minute. 'You used to be such a free spirit. I mean, as a child. Then when Esther got bad...' Her voice trails off. 'Come here,' she says.

They stand in the kitchen with their arms around each other, rocking each other gently, backwards and forwards. Just like they've always done. Just like Esther did.

* * *

The sky has turned a deep blue, as dark as it ever gets in July, although the bonfire makes it look darker than it really is. Esther is sitting with her back against the apple tree, looking up into its branches. Her face comes and goes through the smoke and sparks of the fire. A man wanders over and sits beside her.

Lauren leans further out of her bedroom window to look at the man. She hasn't seen him before, but then she hasn't seen half the people here tonight before either.

'You took my picture earlier,' Esther says to him.

'Oh yeah, sorry about that.' The man grins at her. 'It was when you were hugging the tree. There was a nice contrast

*between your face and the trunk. I mean, texturally.' He
takes a swig of beer.*

'Bullshit!' laughs Esther.

'I'm into photography,' the man adds.

'Double bullshit.'

*Someone is passing round a joint. Esther takes it in her
right hand, leans against the tree and lifts it to her mouth.
She takes her time, inhaling slowly through half-closed eyes.
Then she inhales again.*

'Want some?'

*'Thanks.' The man takes the joint from Esther and inhales.
Then he leans over and passes the joint to the person on his
right. 'So why are you here?' he asks Esther. 'I mean, is this
your place?'*

*'An inheritance. An aunt who never had a family. I was
the named heir in her will.'*

'Lucky you.'

'Because?'

'Because now you don't have to go anywhere, ever again.'

'Exactly.'

'And your friends...?'

'My retinue? Oh, they only appear in the summer.'

'Seasonal hangers-on?'

*'Like you.' Esther closes her eyes and opens them again.
'What's your name, anyway?'*

'Dylan.'

'Pleased to meet you, Dylan.'

*But watching from the safety of her bedroom, Lauren
doesn't feel pleased. She doesn't like Dylan. Not one bit,
though she's not sure why.*

'So you live here alone?' the man called Dylan asks.

'With Lauren.'

'Lauren?'

'My daughter.'

'You're too young for one of those!'

143

'Am I?' Esther closes her eyes again, as if she is going to sleep. Dylan takes the opportunity to stare at her.

'Mummy!' calls Lauren from the bedroom window. 'Mummy!'

* * *

It turns out there are many stages of grief. Natalie, Lauren's counsellor, outlines five: denial, anger, bargaining, depression and acceptance. Then she explains that some psychologists say there are seven stages, or even twelve. Lauren replies that she can only afford five, and the counsellor gently suggests that everything might take a bit longer than Lauren thinks.

Lauren likes Natalie. She's got nice glasses and pink low-lights and a confidence and empathy that Lauren can only dream of. The room they meet in is bright and sunny, with a lime-green sofa and orange cushions and a wooden floor that isn't really wood but looks clean enough to eat your dinner off. There are boxes of tissues strategically placed on the coffee table, as if crying is not a matter of *if* but *when*, which makes Lauren feel better.

'So,' Natalie smiles, at the beginning of their first session. 'Where do you want to start?' It must be the way Natalie says it, because the tears begin immediately. And Lauren tells her. How her mother began smoking dope and went downhill, slowly but steadily, until she was regularly injecting much harder drugs. She describes how Granny had come up to Scotland and taken them back to London; how everything got better for a bit, until Esther started again. And then there was an accident, or an overdose – no one is sure what happened exactly – but suddenly, Esther was gone.

And Natalie listens in a way Lauren has never experienced before. And everything feels not so much like a story as a journey that she and Natalie are embarking on together.

The hour flies by and after fixing the next session, Lauren

heads for home. Granny is out and the house seems too quiet without her. Lauren wanders outside. The area around the back door needs a tidy up. Lauren picks up a broom and starts sweeping the cracked paving slabs. The dust on the slabs rises, revealing a dried-up worm. Lauren pokes at it half-heartedly with her broom but it's stuck to the concrete. Geranium petals fly past like confetti. She stops and watches them. Then she sees a single butterfly wing, stuck to the window. Lauren touches it and it comes off on her finger. The wing is like a miniature sail. Delicate, yet strong.

* * *

It's the oystercatcher that wakes her, flying right over the house. Lauren sits up in bed and looks out of the window. The sun has been up for a while. Lauren checks the clock on the dressing table. The big hand is on the six and the little hand is halfway between the eight and the nine. She jumps out of bed.

'Mummy?' she calls.

No reply.

Lauren goes over to her chest of drawers and yanks the bottom drawer open. She pulls out a vest, a pair of knickers and a clean pair of white socks. Then she takes off her pyjamas and puts on her underwear.

Her school uniform is on the end of her bed where she left it last night, but her shoes are missing. Lauren gets dressed, making sure the school logo is at the front of her sweatshirt rather than the back, then she opens her bedroom door and pads down the corridor.

The curtain has been drawn across the French window in the kitchen and the room is in darkness. There's a terrible smell coming from the living room next door and the sound of snoring. In the gloom, Lauren can make out Dylan lying face down on the carpet. Esther is on the sofa, fast asleep on her back with her mouth wide open.

Lauren tiptoes over to her mother. There is a lot of mess on the floor and Lauren steps carefully over it in her stockinged feet. When she reaches the sofa, she gives her mother a tug. Nothing. Esther is 'out for the count', as Dylan always says. Lauren bends down and puts a hand under the sofa, looking for her school shoes. They're not there.

Back in the kitchen, Lauren opens the biscuit tin. There's half a piece of shortbread lying at the bottom. She lifts it out and tests it with her fingers. Not too soft. The three bears flicker at the back of her mind. Not too hard, not too soft. Just right. Her stomach rumbles.

Lauren needs two hands to open the back door, so she puts the shortbread in her mouth while she wrestles with the handle. Her wellies have been outside all night and she gingerly turns them upside down, hoping there are no spiders inside. Incy, wincy spider. Lauren pushes the thought away and pulls her boots on. Is it gym today? No, not on a Wednesday. Unless it's Thursday. Anyway, her gym bag is in her bedroom and there's no time to get it. Lauren gobbles down her biscuit and runs down the drive to the road.

The school bus is already there.

'No Mam this morning?' the driver says as Lauren clambers up the steps.

She shakes her head. The driver glances towards the cottage. The curtains are closed in the sitting room as if it were the middle of the night.

'She's not well,' says Lauren as she takes her seat.

'Again?' the driver replies. But he sets off without waiting for an answer.

* * *

'To be honest, I've never thought about what I really wanted. I mean, as a career.' Lauren takes a sip from her water bottle. She is glad she brought the water. Having the bottle in her hand is helping. It gives her something to hold on to. And sipping from it is slowing her down and stopping her gabbling too much.

'You were talking about what you really wanted?' says Natalie.

'It wasn't proofreading,' continues Lauren. 'But I don't know what else I could have done...' She takes another sip of water. 'Actually, I did have a fantasy as a child.'

'Tell me.'

'I had this purse. It was white and covered in tiny pearls. Fake ones. And sometimes I used to pretend that every pearl was worth a fortune. And I used to play a game of giving a pearl to people who needed it, like a minted godmother.'

'A secret millionaire?'

'Yes!' Lauren laughs, and then: 'I guess that shows an interest in charity work. But I only played the purse game when we were in Scotland. After we moved to London, I *became* a charity. I mean, we needed help with stuff. School shoes, school dinners, things like that. So there was no way I was going to consider working for one. I wanted to put all that behind me.' Lauren lifts the water bottle up to the light and peers inside. 'It was great going to uni and taking out a loan like everyone else. Feeling like we were all in the same boat. Knowing *everyone* was short of money, not just me.'

'You didn't feel the odd one out.'

'Exactly. And then I noticed that the student union needed a proofreader for the student newspaper. So I volunteered and discovered I was good at it. Then I saw a part-time proofreading job advertised in the local newspaper. I applied and got it, and suddenly I was earning a bit of money, instead—' Lauren swills the water around the bottle and puts the lid back on. 'Instead of having to ask Granny all the time.'

'You wanted to be self-reliant.'

'Yes. Besides, it was great having money. Or at least, not having to worry about it so much.' Lauren puts the water bottle back into her bag. 'Maybe that's why Patrick appealed to me as well. Because money wasn't an issue for him. Or his family.'

'You liked the fact he was comfortable?'

'And not just that. I had this sort of mantra. A kind of wish-list when it came to guys. *Reliable, reputable, respectable.* I thought that was who Patrick was. Turns out I was wrong.'

'You feel disappointed in him.'

'I did at first. Incredibly disappointed. But now, I'm not sure he was what I really wanted anyway.'

'You didn't want someone reliable?'

'Reliable, yes. Respectable, no. Not really. I mean, I thought I did, but...' Lauren glances at her watch. 'I know our hour is nearly up, so we can talk about it another time.'

'Talk about...?'

'Well, I think that if I'd introduced Patrick to Esther, she wouldn't have approved.'

'She wouldn't have liked him?'

'No. And I think I always knew that. Maybe being with Patrick was a kind of knee-jerk reaction to having had a wild mother. But, underneath it all, I knew she loved me more. I mean, more than he ever did.'

'She cared for you more than Patrick?'

'Much more.'

* * *

The car is going so fast, Esther is worried she will hit a pothole. Well, it's a risk she will have to take. She puts her foot on the accelerator and prays. Up the hill she goes, past the sheep and through the wood. It's only when she gets to the fields of barley, harvested now and full of bales, that she sees Lauren. She is marching along the road, on her way to Dornoch. Thank God for the note; thank God she noticed it.

As she draws to a halt beside her daughter, Esther sees that Lauren has remembered everything: her cardigan, her rain mac and her pink and purple rucksack. Although for some reason she is wearing sandals, which feels wrong for the weather. The red patent leather shines in the watery autumn sunshine. At the sound of the car Lauren stops walking, but she doesn't look round.

Esther puts on the handbrake and winds down the window.

'Hi!'

No response.

'Someone was missing you.' Esther picks up the floppy rabbit lying on the seat beside her and waves it out of the open window.

Lauren glances at the rabbit. 'I didn't have room for everything.'

'Of course.' A pause. 'Anyway, well done for remembering your toothbrush.'

Lauren hoists her rucksack further onto her back.

'Although I'm not sure Peter will behave for me,' continues Esther. 'For instance, just now, he wouldn't put his seat belt on.'

'Why not?'

'Because he only listens to you.' Esther doesn't look at her daughter directly, but out of her side mirror, she can see the squall of emotions crossing Lauren's face. She takes her chance. 'I ran away once.'

No reply.

'Do you want to know why?'

Lauren shrugs.

'Granny made me eat tapioca.'

Silence.

'Do you know what that is?'

Lauren moves from one foot to the other.

'It's tadpoles cooked in milk.'

'Tadpoles!' Lauren finally looks at her mother.

'Well, not really tadpoles. Looks like tadpoles, tastes like tadpoles.' A pause. 'It was the last straw.'

'What happened?'

'She caught up with me in the park. Promised never to do it again.'

'And will you *promise*?'

'What if I promise to try?'

'I'm sick of "try".'

There is a rumbling behind them. Esther glances round to see a tractor coming into view. 'What if we ask Granny to come?'

'We don't have a phone anymore.'

'Hamish's mum will let me use hers.'

The tractor is bearing down on them.

'How long can Granny stay?'

'As long as you like.'

Lauren nods and opens the door.

'Move over, Peter,' Esther says, keeping the urgency out of her voice, gently pulling her daughter into the car and driving quickly away. 'Seat belt!'

* * *

After her session with Natalie, Lauren wanders around Croydon, looking for something to take her mind off the greyness of the sky, and then she spots them, hanging in the window of a tiny boutique – a pair of red trousers: tailored, trendy, tight. A clever window-dresser has arranged them so they look as if they are running – a bright pair of legs, bent at the knee. Where are they running to?

When Lauren goes into the shop, a middle-aged woman with short, black hair is totting up the till.

'We're closing.' She doesn't look up.

'But I know what I want.'

'We're open tomorrow, from ten.'

Lauren glances at the legs, running in the window, and she knows she can't wait that long. She looks along the racks of clothes until she spots the trousers in the same red colour.

Amor, says the label. She needs a 12. She rakes through the hangers – 14, 16, 8, 10. But no sign of a 12. Lauren turns to the black-haired shop assistant.

'The trousers in the window – are they a twelve?'

'The red ones?'

'Yes.'

'Yeah, there're a twelve, but there's no time to try them on. Like I said, we're closing.'

'I'll take them.' Lauren can feel heat stinging her cheeks. Where has this impulsiveness come from? She is determined not to leave the shop empty handed; determined that the trousers won't spend another night running on their own.

The shop assistant looks Lauren up and down. 'If you're sure they'll fit…'

The assistant opens a drawer, takes out a pair of scissors and walks over to the window. Then she reaches up and cuts the nylon threads that hold the legs in place. After the first snip, the legs buckle and keel over. After the second, they fall onto the floor of the window display. Lauren holds her breath as the assistant picks them up and brings them back to the till.

'Would you like a bag?'

'Yes please.' Lauren hunts in her pocket for her purse.

'That's eighty pounds.'

It's more than Lauren expected. But also less. As she hands over her card, she realises she would have paid almost anything.

'Enjoy them,' the assistant says as she hands over the bag.

* * *

That night Lauren dreams about Patrick for the first time since they split. A strange dream, because in it she wakes up to find she is in bed with Patrick, but not at his flat in Primrose Hill; instead they are at his father's house. It's early morning and the sun is shining through the windows, creating lozenges of light on the antique furniture. Lauren gets out of bed and looks outside.

From the bedroom, the garden is beautiful. A large lawn, bordered with roses, and beyond the lawn, a line of mature trees. The trees mark the end of the garden and the beginning of Patrick's family estate. A lake, then fields, then moorland beyond.

A blackbird comes hopping across the grass, while in the undergrowth a pheasant whirrs.

'Hey!'

Lauren turns to see Patrick is awake. He looks more attractive than usual, his hair tousled from sleep. He smiles and pats the pillow beside him. 'My father thinks you're marvellous.'

'What do you mean?' asks Lauren, climbing back into bed beside him.

'"Lauren with the lovely legs!" That's what he said to me last night.'

'Is that supposed to be funny?'

'He certainly thought so.'

'Well, it isn't.'

Patrick leans towards Lauren and scoops her hair behind her ear. 'So pretty,' he whispers.

Downstairs, a door opens and a dog starts barking in the garden below.

'My father's Labrador,' says Patrick. 'It loves being outside. Runs for miles if you let it.' He leans towards Lauren to kiss her on the lips.

'It?' Lauren asks.

'She. She runs for miles. We have to make sure we keep the gate shut.'

'Why? There are no roads around here.'

Patrick shrugs. 'She might not come back.'

And then suddenly Lauren is awake. Wide awake.

* * *

The street is deserted. No one around at this hour. Lauren stretches silently on the doorstep before jogging down the garden path towards the front gate.

When she reaches the road, Lauren turns right and starts to go up the hill towards the park. She can feel the surprise in her legs. How long has it been? Months since she charged along the shore of Loch Fleet. Years since she has run in London. And yet there is something strangely familiar about the hard surface of the pavement, the jolt of concrete on her feet and shins, moving up to her knees.

At the top of the hill, Lauren swings into the park and swaps concrete for grass. There was a sharp frost last night, and this morning the ground is as hard as the pavement.

As Lauren crosses the park, her legs seem to lengthen. She had started off feeling jerky and stiff, like a clockwork toy in need of some oil. Now everything is beginning to move with fluidity. She ups her pace and her hair starts bouncing against her back. It feels nice. Reassuring. The weight of her hair beating in time with her feet.

On the other side of the park are shops and a primary school. Lauren lopes past them like a wolf. *Moving, moving. Just keep moving.* A milk float passes with an electric hum. Lauren runs on. More shops, and then a cycle lane. On she goes. She must have covered a couple of miles now. Tomorrow she'll be sore, but she doesn't care about tomorrow. It's today that matters.

CHAPTER 12

The publishing house that has given Nash his big break, not to mention a huge advance, is unusual in that it is based in Edinburgh rather than London. When Nash signed the contract with Few Flies, it felt like a good omen, as if the Scottish connection linked him to Lauren in some way. However, it means that if he needs to have a meeting in person with his publisher, Nash has to jump on a train or a bus.

'Why not fly?' asks his editor.

Nash has no intention of flying. Not only because he wants to save the environment, but also because he is keen to meet the celebrity environmentalist Leonardo DiCaprio.

Yes – Leonardo may be a famous film star while he is only a humble chef, but Nash's publishing deal has given him the feeling that anything is possible. He is sure that eventually, if he keeps refusing to fly and takes a train or a bus instead, then he, Nash Adderman, will come to Leonardo's attention.

This latest trip to Edinburgh is not to see his editor, but his publicist. A man called Jeremy has emailed late in the day and summoned him to a meeting the following morning.

'There's an early flight from Heathrow,' Jeremy said in his email. 'Plenty of seats left, and Few Flies will pay.'

It's ironic, Nash thinks as he boards a night bus to Edinburgh at Victoria bus station, that a publisher called

Few Flies is determined to get him on a plane. Well, not him. Oh no. He won't meet Leonardo that way.

Squashed between a tourist with an enormous rucksack and an old boy in a kilt, Nash imagines embracing DiCaprio in a trendy vegan restaurant. He pictures discussing ethical dishes with his environmental hero. He envisages the two of them baking cakes without palm oil together, then planting hundreds of trees.

Nash clings to his vision all night, but the journey is depressingly long. The tourist with the rucksack listens to loud music through headphones and the man with the kilt falls asleep with his head on Nash's shoulder, and then grunts affectionately in his dreams. As dawn breaks and they cross the border into Scotland, Nash realises that this no flying thing will not work internationally. He will not be crossing the Atlantic by boat – *how long would that take?* – and certainly not by bus.

When he finally arrives in Edinburgh and staggers into the café at the bus station, Nash wonders if Leonardo is really worth it. He adds in David Attenborough. And then a couple of polar bears. But nothing can hide the fact that saving the planet is hard work. A journey that takes an hour on a plane takes ten on a night bus. It's not easy being good. Nash decides that if his book has another reprint, he will add a note about this at the end. An 'epilogue', they call them.

Added to this, the bus is late. Not so late that he will miss his meeting, but late enough that there will be no time to freshen up, as the Americans like to call it. As he chomps through his tofu breakfast burger, Nash wonders if there is a slight tang in the air. The question rears its head again when Nash gets into a taxi to take him to the publishers and the driver shuts the window between the cab and the back seat. And also when the receptionist at Few Flies asks for proof of identity.

'Um...' Nash gets out his railcard. 'It's about a decade out of date, but...'

'How about a driving licence?'

'Don't drive,' says Nash proudly.

'Right,' says the receptionist. 'I'll warn Jeremy you're here.'

When Nash knocks on the door marked MARKETING and lets himself into the office, his publicist is trying to open the window.

'That's the problem with air con,' Jeremy says. 'No chance of natural air.' He gives up trying to open the window, crosses the room and shakes Nash's hand. 'Just arrived? No time to...'

'Freshen up?' Nash says helpfully. 'I arrived late. You see, I came on a bus.'

'A bus!' Jeremy looks amazed. 'You took a bus from London?' He looks Nash up and down, taking in the denim shorts and shirt, the flip flops and the hairy toes. 'Wearing that?'

'It's what I always wear,' says Nash.

'What you always *wore*,' says his publicist. 'Let me tell you, Mash, your image is about to change.'

'It's Nash,' says Nash.

* * *

Shopping for Nash's new look takes the whole day. Mainly because Jeremy and Mash, as the publicist keeps calling him, can't agree on anything. As a vegan, Nash refuses to wear wool. He won't buy anything that needs dry-cleaning, and leather is out of the question. As Nash's self-appointed stylist, Jeremy won't agree to anything that looks suitable for a demonstration, sit-in or pop festival.

They make an unusual duo, Nash thinks, as he emerges time and time again out of curtained changing rooms, only to see his publicist shake his head. Nash in his hippy attire;

Jeremy with his shaved head, blue-rimmed glasses and cashmere sweater. Nash explains he is a denim fan. But Jeremy insists that denim is not only last year, it's last century too.

Eventually, in Harvey Nichols, the author and his publicist find some clothes that they both like. They buy smart but trendy outfits made of seaweed and also hemp, which Nash discovers is both soft and sustainable.

Finally, they are done and back at the coach station in time for the night bus to London. Nash is weighed down with shopping bags – canvas, of course, rather than plastic – and some very expensive sandwiches.

'What a pity we didn't have time for your hair, Mash,' Jeremy says.

'My hair!' exclaims Nash, 'What's wrong with my hair?'

But the driver is shouting 'All aboard!' and Jeremy is pushing Nash onto the bus and then the bus is making its way through the cobbled streets of Edinburgh and out onto the A68 heading south.

* * *

Patrick is not the sort of person who looks back. As a lawyer it would be madness. And as a man, well, it would be pointless. Patrick's father recently had his seventieth birthday party. A great night, which ended with everyone singing a drunken rendition of *My Way*. The song seemed to sum up his father perfectly, and Patrick hopes it will sum him up too. When the time comes.

There is just one line that doesn't sit well with Patrick. The line about regrets. It undermines the whole song, somehow, and Patrick refused to sing the line at the party, taking the opportunity to have another swig of champagne while his father's friends gave it laldy. Patrick has no time for regrets. Which means he hardly misses Lauren at all.

Hardly. Another interesting word, carrying with it a tinge of irony. Because there are times, like when he lights the candle on his bedside table, makes the goodnight pot of Lapsang Souchong and slips into his Paisley dressing-gown, when Patrick does miss Lauren. For a minute, perhaps. Or two. He's not counting. And Veronica doesn't notice. She's usually in the shower when it happens, so Patrick takes the opportunity to walk out onto the patio and remember.

It's nice to have these private moments, so Patrick peeved when one night there is a knocking at the front door which disturbs his contemplation.

It's much too late for a visitor. Patrick hopes the caller will give up and go away. Unfortunately, the knocking comes again. Patrick sighs and goes to answer.

On the doorstep stands a man, smartly but trendily dressed, with an anxious-looking face.

'I don't mean to disturb,' says the man. 'I know it's late, but... I would like to speak to Lauren.'

'I'm sorry, but... who are you?'

'Nash. Nash Adderman.'

'Nash! I didn't—'

'I'm sure she doesn't want to hear from *me*, but...'

'Well, she's not here.'

'Not back yet?'

'She doesn't live here anymore.'

'Why not?'

'Patrick!' calls Veronica.

'Because we are no longer...' Patrick hesitates, '...an item.' There is an awkward silence. 'We haven't been for ages. How did you find me?'

'The phone book, believe it or not. You're still in there. The only Patrick Mounder in Primrose Hill.'

'Well, Lauren's not here.'

'Do you have a contact for her? It's just I paid her back some money and, well... I wanted to be sure she'd got it.'

Patrick shakes his head. 'I don't know where she is.' A

pause. 'She changed her number.'

'Yes, she did.' A pause. 'Well, you must know where she works...'

'Not anymore. I mean, she doesn't work there anymore.' Patrick coughs uneasily. 'Which means I can't help you.'

'What about Granny?'

'Granny?'

'Amelia. Where does *she* live?'

'I've no idea. Somewhere in Croydon.'

'You don't know where Lauren's grandmother lives?'

Patrick shrugs. 'Not the exact address.'

'You've never been there?'

'No.'

'Patrick, I'm waiting!'

'Not even for Christmas?'

'Nope.' A pause. 'Can I ask *you* a question, Nash?'

'Yes?'

'What happened? I mean, you look almost respectable now.'

'Oh, that.' Nash turns and starts lumbering away.

Patrick stands and watches him leave. He thinks Nash seems very sad.

'I say,' calls Patrick. 'You could try Jerbil Publishing. Where she used to work. They might know.'

* * *

Cracking Courgettes

Many people turn to cooking for solace. After a frustrating day, a warmly lit kitchen can provide a sanctuary from the woes of life. If I am feeling upset about anything, I find that messing around with my pots and pans allows me to let off steam!

Today I am going to introduce you to the courgette. A wonderful vegetable – long and firm and the most beautiful colour. I have a friend who works for a paint catalogue and is responsible for naming different paint shades. I always tell him that naming shades of vegetables would be more creative. Exactly what kind of purple is an aubergine? Ink? Velvet? Starry sky? And as for a courgette, its green is so bright and verdant it reminds me of a rainforest.

This recipe only needs two courgettes. It's not a meal for friends; it's a treat just for you. It could be eaten as an appetiser, or even a midnight snack.

Ingredients
A blob of vegan spread (something creamy like coconut)
2 courgettes, chopped
Chilli powder
Lemon zest
Sea salt and freshly ground black pepper

Wash the courgettes, but do not peel. Slice them down the middle and then cut the lengths diagonally into bite-sized pieces.

Cook the courgettes in a steamer for two minutes along with the lemon zest, until the courgettes are al dente.

Heat a blob of vegan spread in a frying pan, add the chilli and sauté the courgettes until the fleshy side is starting to go brown and bubbly.

Tip the courgettes onto a plate, add some sea salt and freshly ground pepper. Now enjoy! Bon appétit. It's time to look after YOU.

* * *

The café at the British Library is empty. Lauren helps herself to a cup of tap water and sits down in a corner to wait for Camilla.

While she waits, Lauren looks around at the towering bookcase that lines one side of the café. It is six storeys high and each storey has four shelves on it. The books are tall, too – old books in leather bindings. It seems a good place to meet her ex-publishing colleague.

Lauren quickly checks her phone. No messages, so Camilla must be on her way. Lauren settles back in her seat, enjoying the quiet. A strange sort of quiet, with a hum behind it – the hum of thoughts and ideas.

'Lauren, you look amazing!' Camilla is striding across the café towards her. 'It's so good to see you!' She gives Lauren a hug.

'So do you!' Lauren glances at her friend. Camilla's hair is no longer blue; instead it's a rather beautiful orange, the orange of a marmalade cat. 'Lovely colour.'

'You don't think it looks a bit rusty?'

'It looks fab.'

'Thanks!' Camilla drops her bag on the floor and flops onto a plastic seat. 'I am so knackered.'

'Let me get you a coffee,' Lauren smiles.

'Make it a double!'

Lauren orders a double espresso and a latte at the counter, and two chocolate brownies.

'I'm not allowed those,' says Camilla when she sees the cakes. 'Mind you, it's a special day. Seeing you again.' She cuts a brownie in half. 'How long has it been, anyway?'

'Ages,' says Lauren. 'I left in April last year, soon after the apostrophe incident...'

'Let me just say,' interrupts Camilla, her mouth full of brownie, 'that our new proofreader is not as careful as you.'

Lauren shrugs and smiles. She doesn't care, she realises with relief. She has moved on from Jerbil Publishing.

'So what are you doing now?'

'I'm taking time out,' says Lauren. 'You see, I never really have. I mean, I just went from one thing to another. Straight from school to university, and by the time I left uni I was already proofreading two days a week. Then I joined Jerbil Publishing for... I can't even remember how long. Three years, four?'

'Four. You came just after me.'

'Blimey, four years. So, now I'm... I don't know, taking stock.'

'Well, it suits you. You look... different.' Camilla smiles at Lauren.

'I'm running a lot. Every day, actually.'

'No wonder you look so good!'

'Thanks. And... I'm getting counselling.' Lauren hadn't planned to tell Camilla, but hey, why not. She was trying to face life head-on nowadays, so why not be honest. Especially with friends.

'Good for you.' Camilla takes a sip of espresso. 'Not because of the apostrophe, I hope!'

Lauren laughs, throwing her head back. 'No! Other things.'

Camilla pauses. 'Someone came into Jerbil Publishing looking for you.'

'Yes, you said on your postcard. Patrick?'

'No, I don't think it was Patrick. Patrick's a lawyer, right? This guy didn't look like a lawyer.'

'How *did* he look?'

'Good question. I mean, his clothes were chic, but his hair was long. Very long, actually. And...' Camilla takes another sip of espresso. 'Imagine a scarecrow in smart clothes. An earnest scarecrow – all smiley and pleasant, but with a worried look in his eyes.'

'Nash...?'

'Maybe. He didn't leave a name. He asked if I knew anyone called Lauren and I said you didn't work there anymore. And he looked like he wanted to ask me a million questions, but then he didn't. He just said thank you and left.'

'You didn't tell him…'

'Tell him what? I only had your address, and I wasn't going to give him that.'

'Did it feel creepy?'

'Not at all. I mean, he didn't insist or anything. Didn't even leave his number. It felt more like… I don't know, Prince Charming trying to find Cinderella. That's why I dropped you that postcard. In case…'

'In case?'

'In case you wanted to be found.'

Lauren gently shakes her head.

'That's what I thought,' says Camilla. 'I probably wouldn't even have contacted you about it, but then, the very same evening, I saw the guy on the telly!'

'Don't tell me, *MasterChef*?'

'Something like that.'

'And how did he look on TV?' Lauren ventures. *Nervous?* she wonders silently. *Confident? As if he has a girlfriend?*

'Unhygienic!' Camilla cries. 'I mean, the guy seriously needs a haircut.'

Camilla laughs, and Lauren joins in, but she is filled with a sudden irrational worry.

* * *

On her way home from the British Library, she sees him on the train. It's too strange; Nash appearing out of nowhere just after her meeting with Camilla. Or, at least, it must be him. He's standing with his back to her, hanging onto a ceiling strap with one hand, holding a newspaper in the other. She can't see his legs to check if he is wearing shorts, because the carriage is packed with people, but he's wearing a denim jacket with MAKE CAKES NOT WAR embroidered on the back. And the hair is exactly like the same – same mousy colour, same bushy texture, same length and everything.

Of course, she could get off at the next stop, before he turns and notices her. But she decides that she should at least say hello, before he disappears into the evening.

She edges nearer, pushing past a man with a briefcase, all the while trying to work out what to say. *What a surprise!* Too false. *What brings you here?* Too formal. *You're looking well.* Too phoney. Perhaps she can just tap him on the arm and let him do the talking.

The train lurches to a halt. The doors slide open and one or two passengers get off. He carries on looking at his newspaper. She is closer now. Almost near enough to read over his shoulder. She lifts her hand, ready to touch him lightly on the sleeve, then she hesitates. *I hear you've got a book coming out. Not that I'm planning to read it!*

As if he senses her, as if he can hear her thoughts, he turns; the man she thinks is Nash. But it's not him after all. It's an older bloke with a lined face and a handlebar moustache.

The train stops again and Lauren stumbles past the man that isn't Nash and onto the platform, even though this isn't her station. When the train leaves, she sinks down onto a bench and stares at the empty track. *No*, she tells herself, she is not disappointed. She is absolutely not disappointed.

* * *

'I just want it washed.' Nash smiles uneasily at his hairdresser. At the same time, he silently curses his publicist. Jeremy is the one who has insisted on him having a 'consultation' with the most expensive stylist in London.

'We're counting down to your book coming out now,' Jeremy had said. 'Just a few weeks to go, Mash. It's important that we get your image just right. You need to lose the hippy look.'

'But then I won't look like me.'

'Exactly,' came the reply.

And rather than dropping the idea, Jeremy booked Nash into a trendy salon in Knightsbridge, with giant cactuses and coffee machines and mirrors surrounded by lights.

So now Nash is confronted with Gareth, who, Nash is horrified to notice, has almost no hair at all.

'It's in terrible condition,' says Gareth. 'At the ends.' He picks up Nash's ponytail and inspects it. 'Split-end city,' he adds. Gareth runs the ponytail through his fingers. 'And not just the ends. Normally, when someone goes for a big chop we suggest donating it, but in your case, well... probably not.'

'Chop!' Nash is horrified. He feels like Samson. A mythical giant who needs to protect his superhuman strength.

'And then there is the... unfortunate whiff,' says Gareth, raising a lock of Nash's hair towards his nose.

'Whiff?'

'A smell of bonfires.'

'Fire-walking,' corrects Nash.

An image pops into his mind. A group of drifters sitting in a smoky room, all with long hair. He turns back to Gareth.

'How would you cut it?' asks Nash.

'Well, we could start by chopping it off above the rubber band.'

'What about below it?'

Gareth sighs impatiently. 'Above, below. Whatever.' And he picks up his scissors.

There is the sound of metal blades working their way through undergrowth. Then, a thud on the floor. 'I don't want to see it!' wails Nash.

'So shut your eyes,' says Gareth, and beckons to an assistant. 'Take it away,' he whispers.

Nash wonders whether he should have kept the ponytail. He could have used it as a dreamcatcher.

'And... open your eyes,' says Gareth. He smiles at Nash in the mirror and flicks Nash's bobbed hair around. 'Now, are we keeping it styled as curtains, or shall I carry on cutting?'

'Keep cutting,' gulps Nash.

Twenty minutes later, and no one can believe the transformation. Washed, styled, moussed and blow-dried, Nash's hair is positively bouncing.

'What do you think?' asks Nash.

'Ha!' cries Gareth, in a way that reminds Nash of Granny.

* * *

When Nash gets home from the hairdressers, it quickly becomes obvious that his basement flat in Vauxhall does not go with his new look. The teepee permanently erected in the sitting room for morning meditations; the elephant turd on the window sill, a souvenir from a month in an Indian ashram. The props that defined and supported his hippy lifestyle would have to go, now that his hair looked like – Nash checks his reflection in the bathroom mirror – like a poodle.

He would need proper furniture. Rugs, lamps, coffee tables. After all, there was always the chance that a journalist would want to interview him 'at home'. Nash has seen these sorts of features in newspapers. A photo of the celebrity in a large conservatory, their feet up on an enormous sofa and their arms around a luxurious-looking cat. Nash doesn't have a sofa. He doesn't even have chairs. He has plenty of saucepans, but they can't sit on those, and his bedroom boasts only a hammock.

For a few moments, Nash mourns his carefree lifestyle. Then he picks up his wallet and walks into town.

* * *

'That will be one hundred and twenty-five pounds,' smiles the shop assistant.

'How much?'

'One hundred and twenty-five,' she repeats.

Nash looks at the bright blue table lamp he is holding. It's attractive, yes, but it seems like an enormous amount for a bit of pottery and a light bulb.

'It's cheaper in other colours,' says the assistant. 'We have it in white for half the price.'

'I'll take this one,' says Nash. *Ridiculous*, he tells himself, buying a lamp in turquoise, when there is absolutely no chance that the woman who loves turquoise will ever see it. But if he is going to spend a fortune on furniture, it will have to be for *her*. He can't imagine anyone else in his sacred space, as he likes to call it.

'If you like the colour,' smiles the assistant, 'we have tableware to match...'

* * *

Although Lauren only started running in the Autumn, it feels like she's been doing it for ages. It's January now; the parks are almost empty and she can leave the paths and jog across the grass. Leaves crunch under her feet.

The changing seasons have helped Lauren to process and running gives her time to think. It's nearly a year since she caught Veronica wearing her bathrobe. And all that time, Nash's book has been moving slowly towards completion. It will have gone through structural edits, copy edits, line edits and proofreads. Nine months of different processes, like a baby developing in the womb. And the strange thing is that if Nash is the mother of the book, she is the father. She was present when Nash started writing; she was the one who conceived the idea of including recipes. She even came up with the title. But then she disappeared.

Sometimes when she is far from the path, Lauren looks up into the trees and wonders how Nash is feeling. Is he looking forward to giving birth? And how will he manage the process on his own? *I'm not ready yet. I'm not ready yet.* Lauren's feet beat in time with the words in her head. And she wonders if she will ever be.

* * *

Nash often dreams about Loch Fleet. And it's always the same dream. He is walking in a marshy basin beside the shore. Tall dunes tower above him, hiding the sea. He can hear the waves thumping on the sand, but he can't see them. Sharp grasses scratch his legs, boggy ground squelches under his feet. There are wildflowers everywhere. Butterflies hover over a clump of purple milk vetch, a bee lands on a grass-of-parnassus flower.

In the dream, Nash can always remember the names of the flowers, but he can never remember exactly where he is. He knows that *Fois* is not far away, but he can't for the life of him remember how to get there.

Hoping that being a bit higher will give him a better lie of the land, Nash clambers up onto a tussock topped with marram grass. But the coast seems to have moved further away, and the dunes have grown taller during his ascent. Below him, heather sways in the breeze and gorse bushes rattle. The gorse flowers are an astonishing yellow and the air is full of the sweet smell of coconut.

Nash gives up and lies down on the marram grass, letting the grass moths tickle his cheek. He will never find her.

CHAPTER 13

One of the nice things about being an up-and-coming lawyer is that Patrick is often the recipient of corporate hospitality. Which means he gets invited to lots of events. Usually they are sporting events, and Patrick is not very sporty. But the hospitality takes the sting out of things. Instead of slumming it in the freezing stands like most people, Patrick watches rugby from an insulated box, knocking back craft beers and pints of Guinness.

Indoor events are preferable, and Veronica loves opera. Especially when they can spend the intervals quaffing champagne rather than queuing at the bar.

Some invitations are stranger than others, and Patrick has had to turn these down. Shamanic Conversations was a no, along with a sensory re-enactment of the Black Death. And then, just when he thought he'd seen it all, Patrick finds two tickets to a book event in his in-tray.

An evening with Nash Adderman to celebrate the launch of
Vegan Recipes for New Age Men.
25 February 2017, 6–8pm
Jake's Place
Complementary bar

So Nash has done it! Patrick is amazed. And, despite their differences, rather pleased. It could be fun to go along, perhaps even shake the author's hand.

Veronica is less impressed. 'You hated that holiday,' she reminds him.

'I hated bits of it.'

'When is it, anyway?'

'Next Saturday.'

'Then we absolutely can't go.'

'Why not?'

'I booked us a spa day, remember.'

'Oh yes.' A pause. 'Do we know anyone else who might like them?'

'You mean, do we know any vegans?' scoffs Veronica. 'Of course not.'

'You're right.' Patrick slides the tickets into the drawer of his bureau.

That night, just after midnight, Patrick is jolted awake. But of course, he does know someone. Two people actually. Not vegans, but...

He returns to the bureau, finds the tickets and slips them into an envelope.

FOR LAUREN AND AMELIA he writes on the front. He googles Jerbil Publishing and carefully adds the address. Even if Lauren's not there anymore, someone will know where she lives. Just to be sure, he adds IMPORTANT DOCUMENTS – PLEASE FORWARD AS NECESSARY. Then he goes back to bed.

* * *

Strange how she always found it hard waking up when she worked at Jerbil Publishing, but nowadays Lauren is up with the lark. There's so much to think about. Natalie has encouraged her to keep a journal, so she can write down her thoughts and feelings between their counselling sessions. And these thoughts and feelings keep pouring out. At first light, Lauren's eyes ping open, her mind flooded with a new memory, a new idea.

Now it's Lauren who is first awake; Lauren who feeds the birds and puts on the coffee machine. And so it's Lauren, and not Granny, who hears the early-morning thump of the letter box.

Lauren goes through to the hall, picks up the large, typed brown envelope that has landed on the mat and takes it upstairs to open. Inside the brown envelope is a smaller white one. On the front of the white envelope it says *Thought I should send it on. Camilla x.* When Lauren opens this envelope, there is yet another one inside. This time the writing is in block capitals. FOR LAUREN AND AMELIA. IMPORTANT DOCUMENTS – PLEASE FORWARD AS NECESSARY. And inside this envelope are two invitations to the book launch of a certain Nash Adderman's debut publication.

'Who the hell...' says Lauren out loud.

'Who the hell what?' Granny has appeared in the doorway. 'What's in the envelope?'

'Nothing.'

'Is it tickets for Nash's book launch?'

'How do you know?'

'I saw it advertised in the paper. How many do we have?'

'You're not going!'

'It would be rude not to.'

'No, Granny. *No!*'

'If you don't go, I will,' says Amelia

'Are you threatening me?'

'It's not a threat, it's a fact.' A pause. 'I might even wear a hat.'

* * *

'So you're not sure what to do?' asks Natalie.

'No.' Normally Lauren loves her counselling sessions. But today she feels almost impatient with Natalie. It's all very well, this active listening that her counsellor does so well, but sometimes Lauren wants Natalie to tell her what to do, not reflect her indecision back to her. 'I mean, I know what I'd like to do...'

'Which is?' Natalie leans forward encouragingly.

'I'd like to forget all about it. Him, rather. It's still possible. I could throw the tickets away.'

Natalie opens her mouth and then closes it again.

'Please don't reflect that back,' Lauren mutters. 'I know what it sounds like, I just don't want to address it yet.'

'Forgive me,' says Natalie. 'But I'm not following. This Nash with the book launch, isn't he the same Nash that squatted in your house?'

'It's all his fault,' Lauren says. 'As usual.'

'You think that he is to blame.'

'I do. And not just for this. For everything. He's the one who started quizzing me about Esther, and the one who looked at the photos. The one who appeared on the radio with absolutely no warning. And now these tickets, arriving out of the blue. Just when I thought I was safe.'

'You thought you were safe? Lauren, I'm confused. You've hardly mentioned Nash before today.'

'I mean, it felt like I was getting everything sorted out. All my emotions – aired, ironed and put away again.'

'But perhaps life isn't quite that simple,' Natalie replies.

'Is that what I said?'

'What you implied, maybe.'

Lauren sighs and shakes her head. 'I still haven't got it, have I? I want to keep my feelings in check. I want to fold them away like laundry. But I can't. Because... they're not even flat.' She is laughing now.

'And is that good or bad, do you think?'

'It's bad, Natalie.'

Natalie is quiet for a moment. 'So, this Nash... he's a hippy, right? And did that bring something up for you about your mum?'

'A bit. I mean, maybe at first. When I arrived at the cottage to find him squatting, with his beard and flip flops and everything, I didn't like it. I mean him. I didn't like him. But then, well… I missed it.'

'Missed it?'

'When he shaved it off. And that's when I realised that it wasn't the fact he was a hippy. It was the fact that he saw me. I mean, he saw the real me. That's what I couldn't cope with.'

'Lauren, I think you need to tell me everything about Nash. All of it. He feels like an important piece of the jigsaw.'

'But I can't, Natalie. I can't even admit it to myself.'

'Perhaps it's time to try.'

* * *

Amelia likes to think that she is *not* stuck in the past. As a grandmother who became a mother overnight, she had to quickly learn the ways of a new generation. Determined not to be the fogie at the school gate, she memorised names of pop groups, or bands, as Lauren called them. She watched films where the action seemed too busy and too fast. She cooked, if you could call it cooking, things that came in boxes and had no taste at all. And she's been able to let go. She's *had* to let go. Not just of people. She's let go of things as well.

But there's one thing she still misses every day. And that's Woolworths. Today is no exception. As she wheels her tartan shopping trolley past the building that was Croydon's North End branch, Amelia turns her head towards it in acknowledgement. It's her daily nostalgic marchpast. Because you could get anything in Woollies. Things you needed, things you wanted and things you didn't want or need but that you went home with anyway.

When it finally shut, this particular branch was probably the oldest still trading in the world. Amelia feels proud of its longevity. If she were ever to get a tattoo, *pigs might fly*, it would probably be of that. A big W, and then the dates.

It was a good quiz show question too. So good that she'd actually sent it in to *Pointless*. The question hasn't come up yet. But it will. Which branch of Woolworths traded the longest? When she is washing up, or peeling potatoes, Amelia adds in other towns as spoilers. *Cheltenham. Chatham. Chester.* It would be fun if they all began with C. More distracting. But she didn't suggest this to whatshisname. He'll do it his way.

Perhaps it's the longevity of the shop that makes its absence such a hole in her life. Because it was around for three childhoods: her own, her daughter's and her granddaughter's.

Imagine a store lasting nearly a hundred years. Amelia doesn't intend to last that long. Now she's eighty-five, things are already falling apart. She'll stick around for a bit, though. Make sure Lauren's ok.

'Watch out, missus!' A car passes, very close to her. Amelia jumps back onto the pavement. How had that happened? *Concentrate.* Right, what's next? Ah, yes.

Amelia hoicks her trolley down the steps leading to the public library. The automatic doors open and she steps into the foyer. The foyer walls are lined with dozens of posters of things to do. That's what she loves about living in London – all the possibilities. Not that she ever does anything, but it's fun to have a browse.

When she is finished looking, she approaches the enquiry desk. 'Excuse me!' Amelia taps a librarian on the arm. 'I'd like to order a book.'

* * *

Granny-Friendly Muffins

It is a truth universally acknowledged that grannies and vegans do not fit naturally together. However, in this chapter I will endeavour to show how even feisty grandmothers born before the Second World War can be won over.

And perhaps it's this war connection that makes grannies convertible. Because they can remember their own mothers substituting one ingredient for another. With essentials rationed until the 1950s, what else could a home baker do? In this recipe, we will replace eggs and butter with a new ingredient: apple cider vinegar.

Yes, I really do mean apple cider vinegar – that bottle you bought from the health food shop because it was on offer but you don't know what to do with. The bottle that, when you unscrew the lid, nearly takes your head off. Believe me when I tell you that this vinegar is marvellous: great for marinades and dressings, pickles and sauces (see page 101 for my Cuban Fiesta recipe).

Like all vinegars, apple cider vinegar is – well, vinegary. And, let's face it, so are grandmothers, at least on the outside. But put some vinegar in my recipe, and it works like magic. The acidity of the fermented apples helps to make the muffins sweet on the inside, rather like grannies themselves.

Ingredients (makes a dozen Granny-Friendly Muffins)
250g/9oz self-raising flour
1 tsp baking powder
250ml/9 floz soya milk
1 tbsp apple cider vinegar
150g/5oz sugar
150g/5oz blueberries or vegan chocolate chips

Preheat the oven to 180°C. Line a muffin tin with 12 compostable baking cups.

In a large bowl, mix together the flour, baking powder and sugar. Add the soya milk and apple cider vinegar. Stir in well. Now fold in the blueberries or vegan chocolate chips.

Fill the baking cups about two-thirds full with the sticky mixture. Bake until a knife inserted into the centre comes out clean. Find a granny to feed them to!

Where would we be without grannies? Good-humoured and resilient, always there in a crisis. Honest and direct. The right kind of sensitive. Knowing when to pipe up and when to keep quiet. Surely they deserve a few muffins?

* * *

All the way through the very expensive spa day, Patrick feels distracted. He knows that wellness is all about being in the 'here and now', but his mind keeps pulling him back to Lauren. Perhaps it's the watery soundtrack washing through the whole spa that reminds him of Loch Fleet. A regular pulse of waves, rolling over and over.

He is sure that the spa has chosen the wave sounds to soothe, but Patrick doesn't find them relaxing. *Will she go?* the waves seem to be saying. *Will she go?*

Patrick doesn't tell Veronica about his agitation; she wouldn't be pleased. Today is her treat, and an expensive one at that. But he can't do it justice.

As the masseuse – soft hands, short fingers – pummels his back, Patrick finds himself hovering over Jake's Place, like a buzzard riding the breeze. *Will she go?* he wonders.

'And over onto your back,' says the masseuse.

'Is it possible to turn off the music?' Patrick asks. 'At least for a bit.'

'Sorry?'

'The muzak. It's kind of annoying.'

'There is no muzak, Mr Mounder.'

'I mean the soundtrack of waves. It's been going on for a while.'

'There is no soundtrack, I'm afraid. No waves in here.'

'Oh. Right. It must be water in my ears. From the pool.'

Except he hasn't been swimming yet.

* * *

'How do I look?' Lauren strides into the sitting room and stands next to Granny.

'Think of the most attractive person you know, then double it,' says Amelia, not taking her eyes off the telly.

'Do you think the jumper goes?'

'I'm watching *Dancing on Ice*.'

'Granny!'

Amelia's eyes swivel round for a nanosecond, before returning to the television. 'Always the same blue,' she sighs. 'But I like the red trousers. Where are you sitting?'

'At the front, unfortunately.'

'Good,' says Granny. 'Very good. Say hello from me.'

* * *

'All done.' Esther places the scissors on the kitchen table and puts the tiara back on her daughter's head, positioning it slightly lopsided, to disguise the uneven fringe. 'There – you look like a princess!' She shows Lauren her face in the mirror.

'It's not straight,' says Lauren. But she doesn't seem to mind. She bounces up off the chair, picks up Peter Rabbit and skips out of the kitchen onto the veranda. Esther follows.

'Look, Granny, I'm a princess!'

Amelia looks up from her knitting. 'I can see that.'

'Come on, Peter.' Lauren skips down the steps of the veranda and into the garden.

'I should have cut it,' says Amelia, when Lauren is out of earshot. 'Your hands are shaking today.'

When she reaches the end of the garden, Lauren turns and waves. Her slanting fringe makes her look even prettier.

'Not as far as the beach!' calls Esther. 'Not on your own.'

'But Peter wants to.'

'No, he doesn't,' Granny replies. 'He wants to stay by the tree.'

Lauren holds the rabbit up to her ear. 'Peter wants to swim to Norway.'

'Does he have a passport?'

'Rabbits don't need them,' says Lauren, in an I'm-tired-of-explaining voice. But she comes back towards the tree, puts Peter on the grass and starts covering him with leaves. 'Go to sleep, go to sleep,' she sings to the rabbit.

'Do you ever wonder...' Esther begins.

'Who her father is?'

'No. Not that.' Esther hesitates. 'I mean about when she's older. Who could ever be good enough?'

'Ha!' laughs Amelia. 'Knit one, purl one,' she adds to no one in particular.

Esther bites her lip. 'If I'm not around, will you...' she pauses, searching for the right word, '...check?'

'Oh, Esther! You've made me drop a stitch.'

* * *

Lauren gets to Jake's Place early. She has this terrible feeling that if she arrives just before it starts, she will bump into Nash in the foyer.

The venue is already thronging with people all talking about veganism and saving the planet. Everyone looks trendy and smart. These are not yurt-dwelling New Age types; these are fashionistas with jobs in the media. These people are already successful in their own right. And yet they want more. They want to meet Nash.

The book has its own table, just inside the doorway. On the front cover is a photograph of a pestle and mortar on a windswept beach. Underneath, in bold type, it says *Vegan Recipes for New Age Men.*

The back cover displays quotes from various chefs and food critics full of praise, like 'Marvellous' and 'memorable' and 'metamorphosis'.

Lauren opens the book and glances at the index. As far as she can work out, Nash has written twenty different chapters for twenty vegan recipes. Before the list of ingredients, he has added his own thoughts. Thoughts on his life, his accident, and – please God, no – even his thoughts on love.

Lauren starts to close the book, ready to put it back with the others. As she does, her eye catches sight of the dedication at the front. *For Lauren, with thanks.*

'Would you like to buy one?' asks an assistant.

'No way!'

The assistant laughs. 'Well, that's refreshingly direct!'

'Thank you,' says Lauren. 'I'm working on it.'

She gets out her ticket and heads for the auditorium. The usher hasn't arrived, but the door is open and Lauren slips inside. The theatre is in darkness, but there is a light on the stage where two men are sitting at a table. One is sporting a shaved head, the other has a bouffant kind of haircut: feathery, fluffed up layers that shine under the light. 'One two, one two,' he says into a microphone.

Lauren stares at the man with the puffed-up hair. 'Nash?'

'Lauren!'

It's definitely Nash's voice, but the rest is unrecognisable. His denim shorts are gone, replaced by expensive trousers, while his flip flops have been traded for black converse trainers. His corduroy shirt looks too smart to be comfortable, and as for his hair...

This strange new Nash jumps up and trots down the stage steps towards Lauren. When he reaches her he holds his arms out, then thinks better of it and puts them back by his side like a heron folding its wings away. 'I can't believe it's you!' he beams.

'And I can't believe it's you, Nash. I mean... what happened?'

'I wrote a book!'

'I mean what happened to *you*?'

Nash runs a hand through what's left of his hair. 'Oh, that,' he says uneasily. 'You don't like it?'

Lauren hesitates. 'No.'

'Why not?'

'I liked the old Nash.'

'I'm still the old Nash,' says the new Nash, but he looks disappointed now.

'Hello!' The man with the shaved head has joined them, a curious smile on his face. 'I'm Jeremy, Mash's – I mean Nash's – publicist. And you're...?'

'Lauren.'

'Oh my God. You're *Lauren*!' cries Jeremy. 'Thank you so much for buying a ticket.'

'I didn't.'

'Didn't?'

'I didn't buy a ticket.'

'Oh,' says Jeremy, but he smiles at her anyway.

'Well, you seem to have a ticket,' says Nash. 'Where are you sitting? B10?' He starts to lead Lauren to her seat.

'I miss the beard, too.' She had to say it; she absolutely had to say it; couldn't stop herself saying it. And now Lauren desperately wants to go home, but Nash has her by the arm and is walking her to the front. *Why did I say 'miss'?* Behind her, Lauren can hear the auditorium filling up. If she tries to leave now, she will have to battle her way past people coming in. They are like the tide filling Loch Fleet, but she is a seal. She could swim against them.

'It's so great to see you,' Nash says, when they reach

Lauren's seat. 'Perhaps afterwards we could…'

'Granny says hello,' Lauren replies.

'How do you, um… feel about everything?' Nash asks warily.

'How do I feel?' Lauren begins. 'Tired. I mean, I haven't slept properly for months. Not since our row, really, although the missing apostrophe didn't help.'

'Apostrophe?'

'But the worst bit was hearing you on the radio.'

'I'm so sorry, Lauren. All those things I said…'

'It's ok. I'm running again now.'

'We're going to start shortly.' Jeremy has appeared at Nash's side.

Nash gives Lauren a searching look, then he turns away, bounding up the stage steps, leaving only his smell behind, a blend of mint and cumin. At least that hasn't changed.

* * *

Safely back on the stage, Nash is in turmoil. His first talk, and he is nervous enough. And now here she is, sitting in the second row. She looks more beautiful. More confident. As witty as ever, but there's something new. A wildness, perhaps? *I didn't buy a ticket.* Oh, his heart.

The problem is, she doesn't like him. Or at least not the new him. If only he'd bumped into her earlier, when he still had hair. When he was still hairy, but also famous and solvent. Would that have worked? Nash flips through images of his transformation, from crumpled hippy to crease-free celebrity, trying to find the perfect Nash, the one that could have won Lauren over. But hold on – she misses the beard, too. Which means… she preferred the first Nash, the scrounger with flip flops? The *real* Nash. Oh, his heart again. He's going to collapse, right here, in front of her, everything leading to this. Perhaps she knows CPR? That would be something.

Lauren glances around, looking for escape routes. The entrance is far behind her, but on the left-hand wall, she spies glass doors leading onto a concourse and a road beyond. If Nash gets too much… Right now he is sitting quietly, lost in thought. She can do this.

Finally, the theatre is full and Jeremy opens the session. He thanks everyone for coming and then introduces Nash, not so much as a cookery writer but as a lifestyle guru. Nash smiles modestly.

Jeremy explains that Nash will read from his book before taking questions from the audience. 'So, Mr Adderman. Would you like to start?'

'Delighted!' says Nash. He picks up *Vegan Recipes for New Age Men*, the pages of which have been earmarked with post-it notes of various colours, and opens it. Then he begins to speak.

'I don't know exactly when it happened. Maybe when I arrived at *Fois* and discovered everything was turquoise. Or the first time we met and you insisted that your house was not a house but a cottage. Maybe it was then. Or perhaps it crept up on me unawares. Whenever it was, you changed everything. You intrigued me; you inspired me; you touched me in a way that…'

'Stop!' Lauren hisses from the second row.

Jeremy looks confused, as if this wasn't the reading he was expecting. Nash turns a page of the book.

'And I don't know exactly why. Perhaps because you would kill for your granny. Or because you eat with your eyes closed. And because you sometimes snore.'

'I don't!' says Lauren. She can't help it.

'Gently, perhaps, but definitely snoring. I could hear you through the wall.'

'Are you sure you've got the right bit?' interjects Jeremy.

'Just now,' continues Nash, looking directly at Lauren,

'Just now you told me that you didn't like my hair. And you're right. It's not me. I shouldn't have gone that far. I'd changed so much I didn't know where to stop. I got caught up in a circus and lost sight of myself. But I can grow it long again. I can grow it to Scotland and back, and besides,' he smiles hopefully at her, 'beards grow quicker…'

'What about the recipes?' calls someone at the back.

'Of course,' says Nash, returning to the book. And he turns another page.

'Have you ever seen a woman run, I mean really run. Flying like the wind beside a stormy sea. Wild running, that's what it looks like. You can live like that. And you can cook like that too…'

As Nash speaks, Lauren thinks about the last time she heard these words; about how upset she had been and how it had propelled her into counselling. And she realises that her recovery is Nash's fault too, and she throws back her head and laughs, just like Esther used to. And then Lauren wants to run. Really run. Out into London, into a new life. And who knows, perhaps Nash will follow her.

Lauren jumps up and starts making her way towards the glass doors, pushing past the people on her row, ignoring the tuts and groans. She is not a seal now; she is an orca. She will devour anyone who tries to stop her.

'Please don't leave!' cries Nash. 'You can't just show up and then disappear. Anyway, that's the emergency exit.'

But it's too late. Lauren has barged through the doors and the alarm is ringing and she has kicked off her sandals and is sprinting across the concourse towards the road.

Nash leaps off the stage. He lands on his bad leg and has to rebalance for a second before dashing after her.

And then the audience are on their feet and racing through the fire doors too, and the concourse is full of vegans and everyone is trying to film everything on their phones, because now Nash has caught up with Lauren and, after a brief scuffle, enveloped her in his arms.

Folded into each other like a calzone, Jeremy is typing into Twitter. *See page 233 for this cheese-free recipe.* #Nash

EPILOGUE

It's Veronica who spots her. In the middle pages of the Sunday supplement.

'Is that Lauren?'

'Um... yes, I believe it is.' Patrick peers at the photograph. She is sitting in a sunny garden with Nash Adderman. *Lauren is wearing a linen suit from the company Soundly Sewn*, it says in the caption. The blue suits her, Patrick can't help noticing. Nash looks very different from the last time Patrick saw him. His hair is shoulder-length, and a bushy beard is nestling inside his collar.

Perhaps the most striking thing about the picture is that Nash is looking at Lauren rather than the camera. Only she is looking out. It's very unusual for a portrait photograph, and Patrick wonders how many times the photographer tried and failed to get Nash to *look this way* before giving up and taking the picture anyway. Behind the two figures, Patrick can make out the branches of an apple tree.

The article beneath the photograph is about a film that is being made of *Vegan Recipes for New Age Men* – except, as Nash is keen to point out, it's about the story behind the book. Nash adds that all profits from the film will go towards his wife's charity. *Hold on– does it say 'wife'?* Patrick double-checks, then glances back at the picture before continuing to skim through the text. He reads that Lauren has started a charity which funds counselling for people who couldn't afford it otherwise. *Why?* he wonders. There are no clues in the article, although Patrick is finding it hard to concentrate, his attention returning again and again to the photograph.

Beside him, Veronica is googling *Soundly Sewn* and muttering that she has never bought vegan clothes before and probably never will again, but that Lauren's suit is irresistible.

Patrick closes his eyes. Just for a moment, he can hear the sounds of Loch Fleet. The lapping water of high tide; the croak of a heron taking flight. A grandmother laughing.

ACKNOWLEDGEMENTS

Huge thanks to family and friends who have supported my writing journey and to all those who have helped with this book: Geneviève Anhoury, Wendy Armstrong, Charlie Bissett, Lily Byron, Catalin Filip, Lottie Fyfe, Fiona Mackenzie, Heather Macpherson, Deborah Padfield, Graham, Lucie and Martin Treacher. Also Jessica Angel, Adele Gallagher, Margaret Jappy, Lynne Mahoney and Katrin Shevardina, thank you for your friendship.

Special thanks to Alison Munro, Helen Sedgwick and Wendy Sutherland for your inspiration, support and encouragement.

ABOUT THE AUTHOR

Liz Treacher is a writer and creative writing tutor. She lives in the Scottish Highlands by the sea and is author of *The Wrong Envelope, The Wrong Direction* and *The Unravelling. Vegan Recipes for New Age Men* is her fourth novel.

www.liztreacher.com

Printed in Great Britain
by Amazon

27986892R00118